STRAY CAT BLUES

A MAX PLANK NOVEL

ROBERT BUCCHIANERI

For Nick and Paula.
Always.

CHAPTER 1

My plan was to spend that Friday in late May and then the rest of the summer in peace and quiet, as far away as I could manage from civilization and its discontents.

I was tucked away in my floating home docked at Pier 39, Fisherman's Wharf, San Francisco.

Home is the *Acapella Blues*, a 42-foot houseboat, a refurbished relic from World War II, where it served honorably as a lifeboat.

I was lounging on the back deck, sipping scalding black coffee from a cracked white mug. The air carried the scent of salt and seaweed and fried eggs. The sky was as blue as it could bear and filled with the sounds of squawking gulls and waves caressing the wood and fiberglass hull. Off in the distance, Alcatraz Island loomed in all its shady glory.

Napping and reading, some fishing when the tide was just right, strumming my guitar, and maybe jotting down some notes and words towards what I modestly call "the magnum opus" were all I had on the agenda.

Well, there was Alexandra Stone. She was back in town for the first time in weeks and actually wanted to see me. The woman will never learn. I'd promised her Thai food and dancing, and the sum total of my attention, to say nothing of my affection.

Things were looking up. Life was peachy keen. I knew it wouldn't last, but I was going to savor the moments while it did.

I'd just earned a small boatload of money rescuing the proverbial damsel in distress, enough to pay my boat slip rent and keep me in beans and beef for the next six months. I had no plans to accomplish anything constructive or beneficial for the human race in the foreseeable future.

Alas, as Robert Burns so lyrically summarized in his apology to a mouse:

THE BEST-LAID SCHEMES O' MICE AN 'MEN
  Gang aft agley,
  An' lea'e us nought but grief an' pain,
  For promis'd joy!

I DIDN'T ANTICIPATE THE STRAY MOUSE THAT TURNED UP ON MY dock late that morning. The tapping on my front door, a slab of tarnished oak with a stained glass porthole inlaid with a Knights of the Roundtable motif, took me by surprise.

I don't often get unexpected visitors. I normally conduct my random business meetings at a dark corner booth of the Rusty Root, my friend Bo Fiddler's establishment on Fisherman's Wharf. I try and keep clients, strangers, and other fowl away from my humble abode.

And the visitor herself made it even more of a surprise.

The girl was about ten years old, give or take a few semesters. Ponytail. Brown blinkers. Wearing jean overalls on top of a ratty white sweater with a black shirt peeking out, she had a dark blue skateboard painted with the moon and stars tucked under her arm.

"Hello, young lady," I said. "Can I help you?"

"Maybe," she said.

I stepped aside, waved my hand. "Would you like to have a seat and tell me all about it?"

She nudged her mouth to the left in an inconclusive way but entered my floating domain without hesitation. I motioned for her to sit on a small leather couch propped up against the starboard side of the boat. She sunk back into it, dwarfed. A Raggedy Ann Doll sprung to life.

I held up a single finger to her, went back out onto the deck to retrieve my mug, grabbed a folding chair, and placed it in front of Raggedy Ann.

I sat down, brought the coffee to my lips, sipped, and smacked in appreciation.

"Would you like…?" I paused. What would she like that I might have? "You don't…?"

She looked at me with those big eyes and said, "I'm fine, Mr. Plank. Thank you."

I like a well-spoken kid, an adult-sounding child. I've not a clue as to how to speak to the regular kind.

I gave the kid my best kindly look and waited.

She plopped the skateboard at her feet, took out a well-used Rubik's cube, and her hands went wild while her eyes stayed fixed on mine. After a lengthy silence, punctuated only by the rasps and whistles of the spinning cube, she said, "So you find people?"

"Sometimes." The cube was, within seconds, all white on top, all red on one side, all blue on the cover. It had to be some kind of new nautical record.

"You're big," she mumbled, staring over my shoulder, out at the sky beyond my desk.

I smiled. "Yup."

"How do you do it?"

"I've got this really cool stretcher rack for a bed and every night I crank myself out just a little further and..." I stopped. She was a tough crowd. Instead of the laugh I expected, I got a no-nonsense frown.

"No, silly. How do you find people?"

"Depends."

"On what?"

"Each case is unique."

"Hmm," she murmured, studying me while her fingers started again, scrambling up the cube, then moving again to unscramble, twisting like the eye of a hurricane. *Whish. Whoosh. Whish.*

"Who'd you lose?"

She ignored me.

I let out a long breath through my nose. She's a kid, I reminded myself, trying to reign in my impatience. I drained my mug of coffee.

"You already know my name, which is a little unfair because I don't know yours."

Her eyes flitted around the room, landing on a grouping of photos that Alexandra had taken during a photo shoot in Africa a couple years back. Her fingers continued to worry the Rubik's cube. "I like giraffes," she whispered.

"Me too."

"My name is Frankie," she mumbled.

It fit her. The kid looked tough. Worldly, in a cute rough-and-tumble way, for a ten-year-old.

"Nice to meet you, Frankie."

She did not respond in kind. Her eyes found mine again and bored deep.

"One more time," I tried. "Why'd you come out here to see me? Shouldn't you be in school today?"

She looked up and away, and her fingers paused. She flipped

the cube into the air and caught it by twisting her left hand backward. It plopped into her palm, and she planted the cube between her legs with a loud crack.

She stared at the square of plastic between her legs for a few seconds, then raised her eyes to me. "Mr. Plank, how much do you charge to find somebody?"

"Once again, that depends."

"Mr. Plank, I've got money."

"Frankie, can you just tell me what you want?"

"It's kind of… well. My sister. She needs help."

"With what?"

"Some guys."

Some things never change and never will. Gals in trouble with guys are one of them.

"Tell me more, Ms. Frankie," I said with a smile.

She narrowed her eyes, trusting my smile as much as a honey badger trusts a cobra. "She did a deal with them. Fair and square." She stopped, looked down at her cube, frowned.

A deal with them. Most of the time when someone utters the word "deal" in my presence, it is not a hopeful sign.

"What kind of a deal?"

"Just a deal. Okay?" She glared up at me, narrowing her eyes.

Okay. Had she been a normal-aged person, I would have just thrown her out at that moment, but I tried to take her lack of years into consideration.

"How old are you?"

She looked away, searching Alexandra's safari pictures, perhaps for some other animal she liked. After a long while, she decided it wouldn't be too dangerous to answer my question.

"Twelve."

"Ahhh. What grade is that?"

Again, she looked away. I was asking awfully tough questions, after all.

"I'm homeschooled."

"But what grade would you be in if you weren't?" I was curious for my own edification.

"Sixth grade."

"I see." I paused. A twelve-year-old is a sixth grader. This interview had not been a total waste of time.

"Why don't you just tell me why you came here to see me?"

She closed her eyes, nibbling her lower lip with her tiny crooked teeth. "My sister is… missing."

"And it has something to do with this deal?"

"Uh huh. It has to."

"How long has she been missing?"

She sniffled, sneezed, and rubbed the side of her nose with her thumb in an odd, endearing way. "A week ago yesterday."

"Have your mom and dad called the police?" I already knew the answer but had to ask anyway.

"I don't have a mom and dad. Just Johnnie."

"Johnnie's your sister?"

She nodded vigorously as if her life depended on it.

Her parents, wherever they'd gone, must have had a weird sense of humor, naming their two baby girls after a boy and a girl who kills him for being unfaithful.

"How old is she?"

"Twenty-two."

A big girl then, but still, out there in the City by the Bay, too many big girls and small ones lived on a razor's edge of safety.

"Tell me about the day she disappeared. When was the last time you saw her?"

She tapped the Rubik's cube against the chair, staring at her blue tennies. "Last Wednesday morning. We had chocolate chip pancakes and then Johnnie said she had to go see Vince and Scooter. She said that they were trying to screw her. She said they weren't going to get away with it." Frankie clutched her knees. "I told her not to go. I was afraid. Scooter and Vince are scary. She said she had to or we'd lose our house. We'd have nothing, no place to live, and then child protection would take me away from her. I couldn't stop crying. I just kept telling her no... no..." Suddenly, her eyes filled with tears. She gritted her teeth, regained her composure, wiped away the wetness with the back of her hand, and glared at me, daring me to say a word about her moment of weakness. I took the cue.

"And you haven't seen her since?"

She shook her head emphatically.

"You have no idea where she went or what might have happened?"

"Thursday, I went and saw Vince and Scooter myself."

"You talked to them?"

"They said they hadn't seen Johnnie at all. They were lying, and I told them that."

"What did they do?"

"Scooter hurt my arm." She held up her left arm and twisted it so I could see the fading red bruise that still looked nasty days after it was inflicted.

"I ran away. I didn't cry. I told them they were shit heads and fuckers and that I was going to get them."

Foul language normally doesn't bother me. I occasionally indulge when warranted. But coming out of the mouth of such a young lass, it still has the ability to startle. Such old-world sentiment.

"How did Mr. Vince and Mr. Scooter react to that?"

"They just laughed. But I'm not kidding. If anything happens to Johnnie, I'll kill them both." She bit her lip hard, her face a fierce mask of pain and anger.

"And you think that I can help." I posed it as a fact, not a question.

She nodded, her face still firm, resolute.

"Why?"

"Man told me."

"Told you what?"

She tightened her grip around the cube, tapped it again lightly, repeatedly, against the seat of the chair and mumbled, "You're tough. Fair." She stopped, wrinkled her nose, then spit it out like it was a mouthful of Brussels sprouts, "Good."

Those were three adjectives all right. To my knowledge, no one had called me the latter in many moons. "Who said that?"

"Aren't you?" She peered up at me with suspicious eyes.

I shrugged. I try not to toot my own horn. Anyway, tough, good, and fair are pretty relative qualities. My ex-wife, old buddies, and clients all might well disagree.

"What was the man's name?" I tried again.

Tap tap tapping of Rubik's cube against old wood. A picture of a scrawny woodpecker working an old oak popped into my mind. A fall day, brown leaves floating in the shimmery sunlit air outside my window, a million years ago when I was about the same age as this kid.

Memories light the corners of my mind.

"Poe."

"Poe? Poe in Treasure Island? At the casino?" How did she know Poe?

"Poe," she said firmly.

I didn't like it. Why was she involved with Poe? It wasn't a good sign for her or her big sister. It bothered me and I wondered why.

"Here," she said, digging around in her shirt. She pulled out a creased photograph, stood up, and reached over the desk to place it in my hand.

It was a picture of Frankie, taken in the not-too-distant past, standing next to a tall brunette. The brunette wasn't wearing makeup and didn't need any. She was a sight for sore eyes. I tried to hide my reaction. When I looked up, I thought I detected an accusatory look in Frankie's eyes, but maybe it was just me feeling guilty about my primal urges in front of a little girl who loved the object of my untoward affection in a purer way.

"That's my big sister," she said proudly, almost defiantly.

"It sure is," I said. "You look like her."

Her features softened, her shoulders rose, her eyes relaxing a bit. Once in a while, I say the right thing despite myself.

"I don't usually take missing person cases like this one. I think it would be a good idea to go to the police and see if—"

"No!"

"Frankie, I—"

"No, please, Mr. Plank. You're our only hope. We can't go to the police. Trust me. That would be the end. I'm afraid… Johnnie would kill me. They wouldn't help. They'd take me away. They might put Johnnie in jail." She stopped talking in order to squeeze her eyes shut.

I reached out and put my hand on her knee until she looked up into my eyes.

"I probably won't be able to help, but for sure I can't unless you tell me about what your sister's business was with Vince and Scooter."

She stared into my eyes for a long time. "I don't know," she murmured.

"Frankie..."

She closed her eyes and put her fingers in her ears.

See no evil. Hear no evil. Speak evil truth.

She let out a sigh and started in. "Paintings. She sold paintings and sculptures. She'd order them online. From far away mostly. Then she'd resell them and make money. She'd go out a couple times a week with a painting or two, sometimes a statue, and she'd be gone for most of the day. When she came back, we had money again. Enough so we could pay our rent and buy food, and sometimes we'd go out to IHOP or even to a movie. *The Terminator.*"

I admired her taste in flicks. Arnold's thespian heights can thrill even the most jaded moviegoer.

Maybe I'm a cynic, but I had my doubts about big sister Johnnie and her art dealing business. Having seen her photo, I could guess where the money she brought back home to Frankie came from. Beauty like hers was a valuable commodity. There were men, all too many men—some of them otherwise good men, others rotten to the core—who would trade their souls, to say nothing of their money, to spend a little time with such beauty. To take advantage of a woman at loose ends, with too much responsibility too soon.

But it seemed as if something more was going on here, too. Maybe she was the one taking advantage of the weaknesses of the frailer gender. Whoever was to blame, she'd been double-crossed somehow, and it seemed to be a significant threat to her livelihood. More than sex was involved, although usually, that ingredient could spoil an otherwise perfectly good stew.

I had no idea what the paintings were about. Just a ruse to fool her sister so she wouldn't find out what was really going on? It seemed too elaborate. You could fool most twelve-year-olds with way less time and trouble.

"So Vince and Scooter bought paintings from her?"

"Yes, a big order. Six expensive ones. But she said they wouldn't pay her what they were worth. They just took them and never paid."

"Hmmm," I murmured, mulling that over. "Is there anything else you can tell me about your sister? Or Vince and Scooter?"

She let out a long sigh. "My sister took her gun with her. She said they weren't going to get away with it."

Famous last words. My heart sank. "What kind of gun?"

"I don't know. A small gun, a pistol. She put it inside her jacket."

"And Vince and Scooter. You know much about them? What they do?"

She shook her head, then her eyes widened as she remembered something. "Johnnie said they were Blue Notes."

I raised an eyebrow.

"I don't know what it means. She just said they were Blue Notes."

"Okay. One more question. How do you know Poe?"

"I met him a few times. He seemed like a nice man. He had M&M's, red, blue and yellow. Johnnie said he was a friend and that he helped us a lot. I didn't know where else to go or what to do, so I went to him, and he said to come and see you."

I took a breath of salty air, reflecting on what I'd just heard, catching the unmistakable stink coming off this whole situation. I looked at Frankie again. Something about her I trusted. Not necessarily what she was telling me, because that most likely had little relation to the whole truth, but my sense was that here sat a good kid. Period. She'd seen too much at a young age but hadn't been broken by it yet. She was probably on the verge, though, if things turned out like it appeared they might.

"Can you help us? I can pay. You can trust me." Her look was open, guileless.

Up until that moment, I had no intention of getting involved. But something in those last four words, and, goddamn me, the look on her face when she said that I could trust her, sealed it for me.

"How much money do you have?"

She stood up, shoved her fingers in her front pocket and extracted a bundle of bills in a rubber band. She extended it out to me. "Three hundred eight dollars."

I nodded. Gave her a little whistle to show how impressed I was.

"Why don't you hang onto that for the moment. Let me check around and see what I can find out for you. We can talk about money later after we find out a little bit more. Okay?"

"Okay," she murmured, biting her lower lip. She shoved the money back in her pants.

"Where can I find Scooter and Vince?"

"They have a car garage. That's where I found them last time. It's not too far from where I live. There's a sign that says, 'Good & Plenty Repairs.'"

"Alright," I said. I'd do what I could, which, I thought at the time, wouldn't be much. I'd talk to Poe, check out her story, find out what I could about Vince and Scooter and why they were Blue Notes.

All things being equal, I'd come up with less than nothing and tell the girl the cold, hard truth. Her sister had disappeared for good and she was all alone in the rotting metropolis.

That's what I thought then.

If I had known what was in store for me, I would have given the kid a lollipop, patted her on the head, and ushered her out of my office faster than she could flip her Rubik's cube.

CHAPTER 2

ut on the dock leading to my houseboat, Frankie spun on her skateboard, singing a rap ditty.

BOOTY BOOTY
Plump and moody
Booty booty
Mamma do me

JEEZ.

"Frankie?"

She danced. Pivoting, jumping. Behind me, around me, whirling like the proverbial dervish.

"Did Poe tell you where to find me?"

"Uh huh," she said, continuing to rap.

Booty booty

   Plump and moody

I'D MOVED TO THE BOAT SINCE THE LAST TIME I'D DEALT WITH POE. I wasn't surprised that he kept tabs on me or everyone else in his universe. He was a careful man.

Booty booty—

"POE KNOWS LOTS A THINGS," FRANKIE ADDED. TRULY THE understatement of the day.

I asked how I could get in touch with her.

She seesawed on her skateboard, rocking back and forth, her arms out surfer style. She jumped high, flipped the board end over end, landed back squarely on top of it.

Showoff.

"I'll come by and see you on Thursday."

"How can I reach you?"

She shrugged.

"Do you have a phone number?"

"Nope. Johnnie has a cell phone, but she took it with her."

"Have you called it?"

"Hundred times. It rings, but she doesn't answer. Just recorded Johnnie telling me she'll call back if I ask nicely. I've left ten messages. Sometimes I call just to hear her voice and..."

My hope for the physical well-being of her big sister dimmed as Frankie continued talking.

"...the people in the house upstairs are getting a little cranky about me using their phone every day. I sneak in anyways."

"Where do you live?"

Balancing on the board, still rocking, she again took my measure and didn't respond.

"Look, Frankie. You have to trust me. I can't help you if you don't."

She narrowed her eyes for a moment, giving me the once over twice before her face softened.

"Okay. In the basement of a house."

"Where."

"Mission."

"That's a pretty big area. What's the address?"

"Near the park. It's this big old white house on Church Street, right across the street from Mission Dolores Park. Me and Johnnie live in the basement."

"What's the number?"

She rolled her eyes up, thinking. Then she shrugged. "Don't know. But there's a weather vane on the roof with a chicken on it. A scarecrow too, like in the *Wizard of Oz*, in the middle of a tomato garden in the front yard. When I was a kid, I used to play Dorothy. My cat Leeshiepoo was Toto." She frowned. "Leeshie got run over." She paused, shook her head. "She was a good kitty. Wasn't her fault that she wasn't a dog." Frankie rolled back and forth on her skateboard and mumbled, "Are you going to come and visit me?"

"Maybe. I just want to know where I can find you if I need to tell you something or ask for more information about Johnnie."

"I'll come by again in two days."

"Can I call the number at the house above your apartment if I have to? Can someone fetch you and have you take the call?"

"I guess so..." She wrinkled her brow, scrunching her lips to the right. "Maggie or Leonard will answer. They're a little wacky. Johnnie calls them hippie-dippie. But they're okay. I'll tell them you might call."

She gave me the number, and I scribbled it down on one of my cards.

"How did you get all the way out here to see me?" I looked dubiously at her skateboard.

"The bus and this." She pointed at the skateboard.

"You're pretty slick on that thing."

"My Ollies and Kickflips are pretty good." She hammered the board with her right foot and jumped in the air. The board flipped over, and she landed squarely on it, spun a 360, and said, "Ta-da!"

"Wow," I said.

"Workin' on a nollie. I'll show you when I have it down."

"Can't wait," I said.

Her eyes darkened, a worry flashing over her face.

"What's the matter?"

She locked eyes with me. "You're really going to look hard for her, Mr. Plank?"

"Yes, I really am."

"Pinkie promise?" Her tiny finger extended toward me. I bent my own around it, and we wiggled together. I started to smile but saw she was serious as a stroke and wiped my face clean.

"Or hope to die," she whispered.

"Or hope to die," I repeated.

If there's one thing I take seriously, it's a pinkie promise.

LATER THAT MORNING AS I WAS NEARLY NAPPING OUT ON THE BACK deck with my fishing line dipped in the placid waters of the Bay, there came another rapping at my door.

Tis some visitor, I mused, tapping at my chamber door. Only this and nothing more...

The conversation I'd had with Frankie about Poe was definitely weighing on my mind.

Meiying popped her head out through the back door of my cabin and said, "Plank."

"What brings you on board my vessel at this ungodly hour?"

She and her partner, Dao, rarely woke or ventured from their yacht earlier than noon. Their 97-foot boat, *Sweet and Sour*, was docked in the waters a few hundred yards away from me. Meiying was a thin reed of a woman in her early sixties, with a mane of still mostly black hair fixed tightly to her head. Everything about her was a little too rigid, including her unusual steel gray eyes. I'd seen pictures of her when she was in her twenties and ravishingly beautiful. She still retained a porcelain-like beauty. More importantly, Dao adored her and vice-versa. I couldn't imagine them without each other.

"Dao want you come for dinner. Big party. He make his famous Gunpowder Chicken and Hoisin wraps."

"What's the occasion?"

"New investment opportunity."

"Meiying..."

"I know. I know. You not invest. You not believe. You put all you money in sock and hide it on boat here. I worry for you, Plank. No children. Old age. No nest egg."

"When I'm old and without money, I'll come live on your boat with Dao and you."

Meiying frowned. "We love Plank. Dao loves Plank. We give you money to stay off our boat."

"See? I don't need investments with good friends like you."

Meiying shook her head disapprovingly but held her tongue. We'd had variations on this conversation for the past five years since I'd become friends with Dao.

"You come tonight. Be some nice Asian ladies there."

"I'm not looking for—"

"You should marry Alexandra. But you don't. Stupid. So Meiying find you Asian lady and maybe—"

"You're wasting your—"

"No matter. You come for Gunpowder chicken or ladies or both. Fine?"

"I come for the chicken...and the wraps."

"Good," she said, turned, stopped, angled her face back. "Little girl come see you?"

"How'd you know about her?"

"We dock this morning. Get gas. Little girl ask where she can find you."

"She found me."

"She have trouble," Meiying stated.

I nodded.

"You help?"

"Going to try."

"Good man."

That was the second time this morning that I'd been called a good man. It was starting to make me nervous.

"See you tonight. 8 p.m. Dress sharp. Remember nice Asian ladies."

With that, she turned and left me trying not to think about how nice these Asian ladies might be.

CHAPTER 3

I stopped in at the Rusty Root early in the afternoon hoping to have a chat with Bo Fiddler, who had more experience with Poe than I did. I wanted to see if he had any updated information about Poe's recent activities, if anything had changed, or if he still had his sticky fingers in a variety of meaty pies.

I walked through the dining room and into the kitchen where I found the chef, a young kid by the name of Rope Rivers, I kid you not, lecturing a sous chef twice his age about remoulade sauce.

"Rope," I interrupted.

The both of them looked up, startled for a moment. Rope smiled. "Max," he said. He wore a bandana looped around his slicked-back red hair. He had freckles and rosy cheeks and looked like he was nearing the end of a thirty-day fast. He was twenty-six, but his emaciated appearance suggested ten years older.

"Where's the boss?"

"In hiding."

"With the band?"

"I think so. He's always a little cryptic about his musical interludes."

When he practiced with his on-and-off again band, The Harder You Fall, he shut himself off completely from the real world for hours, if not days.

"When do you expect him?"

"Dinner time, but I wouldn't be surprised if he doesn't show till later. He'll be in, but when he's got the band going, his sense of timing goes off-kilter."

Bo was usually a constant presence in his restaurant, one of the reasons it was so successful. But music was his first love and passion, just like it had been mine. We'd been in the same succession of bands in our late teens and through our mid-twenties, always on the verge of making it.

I left the two chefs to resolve their saucy dispute and left through the back door that led into a large shed-like structure made of corrugated metal that Bo used for storing supplies and other odds and ends. Tucked in a corner of the building beneath a blue tarp was my Ducati Veltro racing bike, a gift from Dao and Meiying on my thirty-ninth birthday last year.

I hadn't wanted to accept it, but I knew if I refused, I'd be insulting them.

It was a piece of work. Looked almost as cool as Batman's ride. All black carbon and magnesium, smooth and supple as a woman's behind. There were less than a hundred ever produced, and it must have cost them a small fortune. I'd been riding an old Honda, and Dao felt like he owed me a big favor because I'd helped him out of a jam with a fellow yacht owner who was docked nearby and making an asshole of himself. Actually, Marsh Chapin had resolved that situation for me in his inimitable and decisive way.

The Ducati was as sleek and sharp as a switchblade, as fast as the blink of an eye.

I rolled the bike out the shed door, locked things up, then settled onto the leather seat and cranked the engine. It rumbled on with a smooth growl that morphed quickly into a powerful smooth hum. I glanced up at the sky, a forever sprawl of sunlit blue, and breathed in the sea-filled air.

In seconds, I was threading through traffic, the sea breeze from the Bay to my right ruffling my hair. I wound around Jefferson Street, then over to Beach and Bay, around Aquatic Park and Fort Mason, and onto Marina Boulevard.

I pulled into the small driveway of Bo's massive, glass-fronted, two-story home, kitty corner to the lovely Marina Green and directly across from the stately boats anchored in Yacht Harbor.

The Marina district is home to some of San Francisco's most expensive real estate, and Bo's house is worth millions. But he isn't really that rich—or he is, but only if he sells the house. The property was left to him by his parents, who bought it for a relative song back in the forties.

As I stepped out onto his driveway, I felt the ground rumbling. For a moment, I thought it might be the beginning of a quake, and I knew that if that were the case, this was one of the worst places in the city to be. The land beneath my feet used to be shallows, tidal pools, sand dunes. In the 1989 Loma Prieta earthquake, the whole area got hammered—the fill liquefied, water mains broke, fires raged.

The moment passed, and I realized the vibrations were caused by the pounding rhythms of the drums and bass guitars coming through the powerful speakers lining Bo's garage.

The dwellings here are attached to each other like townhouses. Amazing, considering what they cost. You can't beat the location though, and that's everything. You don't get much land for your millions, but who needs it with such glorious surroundings?

I knew that he probably wouldn't hear my knocks or rings on his doorbell beneath the rock racket they were making. I tried his cell phone, as I had earlier in the morning, but it went straight to voicemail again.

As I pondered my assault on the house, the din of the music suddenly stopped, and the garage door swung open.

Drumsticks in hand, Bo Fiddler stepped out onto the driveway and flashed me a surprised look. Behind him, the band—Marty on bass, Martha on electric violin, Pete on sax, and Vig on keyboards —fierce middle-aged rockers, all stood in various poses and somehow, as a group, conveyed a feeling of both energy and enervation at the same time.

"Plank," Bo said.

"Sticks," I responded.

We both nodded, grinned.

Bo was wearing polka dot suspenders over a short-sleeved blue t-shirt above a pair of ripped jeans. He was a big man, with big arms and stumpy legs. He had curly black hair that sprawled over his head in a tangled mop. His midsection had slowly, pleasantly, progressed over the years since he'd purchased the restaurant and now was a substantial asset spilling over his belt buckle.

"Got a gig?" I asked.

"My daughter's wedding."

"What?"

He shrugged.

"I didn't even know she was dating."

"Love is like an arrow," Bo said flatly.

"She's what...nineteen?"

"Eighteen."

"Jeez."

"Love has no truck with age."

I hadn't seen Jen for a few months. I remembered her junior prom when I happened to be over for dinner and the sweaty, big-handed boy with the cowlick who shook my hand and giggled like a school girl. I hoped to hell he wasn't the groom.

"One more cliche about love and I'm going to need a paper bag."

"Love means never having to say you're sorry."

I must have looked sick because Bo came over and patted me on the back. "He's a good kid. They're both good kids. I talked to her. I talked to him. It's hopeless. I try to remember what I was like when I was eighteen."

"Does it help?"

"No," he said, rolling his eyes.

"When's the big day?"

"End of September."

There wasn't much else to say about that. I'm not a big believer in marriage at any age, but I have a strict recommendation for any youth foolish enough to ask my opinion—under no circumstance marry before the age of thirty. Even that is merely a lower limit.

Been there. Done that. Got the scars to prove it.

"So?" Bo asked.

I glanced over at the band members. Vig and Pete, the former totally bald, the latter with his long graying hair falling over his shoulders, stood at the keyboard chatting. Marty and Martha, married to each other and usually either fighting or necking in public, were watching us.

"Can you come with me for a minute?" I turned and, dodging traffic, crossed Marina Boulevard. Bo followed, and we stood in front of a one-hundred-plus-foot yacht with a finish that looked like copper glistening in the sun.

I turned to Bo and said, "Have you seen Poe lately?"

He frowned. "He was at the restaurant a few weeks ago."

"What he's been up to? Do you know of any changes in his business, habits, his people?"

"What's going on, Max?"

I quickly summarized my encounter with Frankie. When I finished, he said, "You're taking the case for free?"

"I don't know what I'm doing yet. Just trying to get a little information and see if I can help the kid out."

He nodded, shook his head. "Poe came by with his..." He paused, glanced out at the yacht harbor—seagulls soaring, boats rocking, sunlight glistening off the waves—and winced. "Entourage," dragging out the syllables. "About a month ago. They closed up the place. I dismissed everybody else, and Poe and I had a chat at a side table while his party—eight of them, each a unique evolutionary specimen—ate my food for free."

A few years ago, Bo discovered that Poe was his landlord, having purchased the building which housed the Rusty Root, though the owner of record was an attorney known to be friendly with Poe. There'd been one steep rent increase since then, but other than that it had been business as usual.

"What did he want?"

"Hard to say. I think he likes me." Bo smiled, shook his head. "He wasn't trying to strong arm me. He didn't mention a rent increase. Probably knows I can't pay anymore and still have a viable business. He asked about my restaurant, inquired politely about the gossip in the neighborhood. Told me he loved the food."

"Nothing else?"

"He said that his own neighborhood was 'transitioning.' Said it was all to the good and that his own business was benefitting from the changes." Bo pursed his lips, nodded. "That's about it."

Poe's base of operations was on Treasure Island, a strange, spooky, sparsely populated pile of fill sitting on natural shoals in the Bay. It had been created for the 1939 World's Fair. Poe runs it like his own personal fiefdom, paying off cops and politicians who are happy to turn a blind eye to his pastimes. After many years of behind the scenes political maneuverings, he got approval to build a casino there, and the tax revenues from that keep all the cats in Sacramento purring and declawed.

I stood staring back at Bo's garage for a few moments, mulling existentially the nothingness of what I'd learned.

"You going out to see him?"

"Guess so."

"Be careful, buddy."

I nodded. "Band sounded pretty good from what I heard."

"We suck."

"You'll knock 'em dead. Your daughter and new son-in-law will be the talk of the town."

"Shit."

"That too," I said.

CHAPTER 4

As I crossed the isthmus that connects Yerba Buena Island to Treasure Island, I was aware of the blood pumping in my veins, the thrill of the rumbling bike between my legs, along with a more uncomfortable feeling, a wariness anticipating a meeting with Poe.

On the Avenue of the Palms with San Francisco Bay's waters just feet from my bike, I glanced out at Alcatraz Island and beyond it to the gleaming spires of the Golden Gate Bridge. If there is a better view anywhere in the universe, I have yet to encounter it.

I zipped up around Perimeter Drive with Angel Island beneath a cloud cover looming in the distance. A cruise ship housing thousands of gamblers was moored a few hundred yards out in the bay. A three-masted schooner floated closer in. I guessed it was Poe's boat, perhaps out there only to add flavor.

To my right, the resort complex, Pirate's Cove, spread out like an octopus.

Actually, there was no "like" about it. It was a man-made octopus. Perched at water's edge was the main casino, a gigantic smoky glass round hub with eight curling steel and glass spindles reaching out from it. Two of them held hotel rooms coursing out over the bay and anchored to the ocean floor by concrete hands. Topped by overhanging walkways lush with palms, fountains, Daliesque statuary, even a couple of water slides. And game parlors, where you could continue to lose money while getting your fresh air break from the casino.

It was Las Vegas transplanted to San Francisco.

The design was ridiculous. The architect, Raise Fuhlman out of Hong Kong was an idiot savant. From the start, it seemed a boondoggle of the highest order. San Francisco was much too cosmopolitan for a development of such tacky kitsch.

But, so far, all the prognosticators were wrong. It had been an unmitigated success since it opened a little more than a year ago. Tourists and the home crowd alike flocked to it like seagulls to a rotting whale corpse.

Poe had to be making millions. Of course, for him, enough was never enough.

I pulled into the mouth of the beast via one of the tentacles—a tunnel leading directly into the underground garage beneath the casino.

Bo had told me Poe's base of operations was on the top floor of the casino, eighteen stories high. I figured Poe must be suffering from delusions of grandeur. He belonged in the basement, underground, a black widow spinning his webs in the dark.

I took the metal stairs, my rubber-soled shoes squeaking, to the first floor, opening out into the cacophony of the casino. Dominating the center of the room was a pirate ship, supposedly a replica of the Black Pearl from *Pirates of the Caribbean*.

Slots, blackjack tables, and roulette wheels were strewn all over the deck of the ship and spilled out all around it in longboats and luggers, where the hopeful and the hopeless could nurture the dream of pirate treasure—despite the fact that the machines here were manipulated to pay out even less frequently than those up in Lake Tahoe.

The light was dim, the floor painted sea blue, and the ceiling black with bright starburst patterns.

The tin sound of the slots mixed with the crackle of people laughing, crying out, shouting. The subtle sweet stench of excess spirits (alcohol only one of them) reflected the thrum of the casino itself. The machine of the system was visceral, a sweet sucker punch—it either thrilled or sickened depending on your predilections.

I'd been here once before with Bo when we'd played a few rounds of blackjack and caught a show in the lounge featuring a still blistering hot Steve Miller. It had been a pleasant experience overall. We'd both left with a few dragoons in our pockets and met two lovely women, Katherine and Paula. Both approaching the dangerous age of forty—lifelong friends from Hoboken and Palm Beach respectively—they'd been on a weekend getaway to see if they could recapture a touch of something lost after divorces and other depredations of age. They were kind enough to spend the evening with us. I like to think they recall that night with fond smiles, and maybe a blush or two.

All in all, I had nothing against Pirate's Cove.

Up against the south wall of the place was a reception area featuring islands of sand, palm and coconut trees made of metal, treasure chests, babbling water fountains, comely wax wenches. I engaged a pretty, young red-haired woman behind the black granite desk wearing a Swashbuckler's hat and pirate corset fulfilling the designer's intent. She smelled like the second day of spring.

She flashed a big smile; I returned the favor.

In that brief moment, I felt we connected on a subtle, yet profound level.

She wore a tag that read, "Julie."

"Julie," I said. "I'd like to get up to the eighteenth floor."

She frowned. "Nothing's on the eighteenth floor, sir."

I nodded. "That right?"

"Yes. Do you need a room, sir?"

"I believe the owner of this casino is on the eighteenth floor, Julie."

She looked at me. I looked back. Moments passed. She appeared to be a bit confused.

"I speak of Poe."

Her face dropped. I'd crossed a line.

"Poe," I repeated.

"One moment, sir." She spun and disappeared into a narrow hallway to my right.

It was a full five minutes before she returned, trailed by an older man not wearing a pirate outfit. I took this to mean that this was a more seriously empowered employee.

He stepped in front of Julie and drew a deep breath, puffing up his chest a bit, before giving me a plastic smile. He was around fifty, soft around the edges, a falcon face, big ears, and jet black hair that looked suspiciously like a piece.

"Hello. Dave Robins at your service. How can we help, Mr...?"

"Plank."

"Yes. Mr. Plank."

I wondered why it had taken more than five minutes and Julie hadn't even explained my *raison d'etre* to the man. "Well, Dave, as I explained to Julie, I'd like to see Poe."

"Poe?"

"Yes, as in Edgar Allan."

This was funnier than it seemed if you knew Poe. Dave's lips did not move an iota from their straight professional line.

"Do you have an appointment?"

"Nope. But we're old friends. He'll be surprised and pleased,

I'm sure." He would be surprised, but probably not altogether joyful.

"I see. Wait here a moment, please."

Dave disappeared while Julie stood back from the reception desk staring off into the distance. Our initial chemistry evaporated like a mirage.

Dave never did return.

Two men, with an obvious fondness for free weights and tanning salons, appeared at my elbows. Each placed a large hand on my shoulders, almost simultaneously.

"Mr. Plank," the one tampering with my right shoulder said in a gruff voice.

I turned to look into gray eyes displaying a decided lack of emotion. He was shorter than me but twice as wide.

I nodded.

"Come with us," he said.

"Remove your hands," I said.

"You got a problem?" the man gripping my left shoulder responded. I turned to him. He was my height, slimmer, with a face only a mother could love, and eyes that twinkled darkly when he smiled.

"None whatsoever."

"Then do what the man told you to."

"Love to."

I shrugged, ducked, spun low and away, and turned back to face the men.

"Let's go, gentlemen. Lead the way. I'll follow."

Short and wide attempted to reassert his hand. I slapped it away.

The two men looked at each other, frowns on their faces, consternation in their expressions. I suppose it was relatively rare for anyone to resist their kindly ministrations.

"What do ya think, Art?"

Tall, thin, Art breathed a long one through his little nostrils while sizing me up. "Okay. Forget it, Rex."

"Rex?" I said.

Art turned. Rex followed lockstep. I trailed behind. Three ugly ducklings all in a row.

WE ENDED UP IN AN EMPLOYEES-ONLY AREA, HIDDEN BESIDE THE bank of customer elevators, behind a door that Art opened using a card key. It smelled like lemon cleaner, sweat, smoke, and cooking oil upchucked by a drunken sailor.

Art told me they had to search me. Expecting no less, I nodded my okay, and Rex felt me up.

"Did you enjoy that?" I asked when he'd finished.

"Shit head," he snarled.

I took it as a compliment.

Two service elevators were waiting for us, and I followed them into one. They spread out on opposite sides, forcing me to take up the middle position.

"Is Poe a fun boss to work for?" I asked as the elevator began humming upward.

Art chuckled but said nothing.

That was the extent of the small talk.

The elevator stopped on the seventeenth floor, one short of our expected destination. Art's hand came up toward my elbow, then wavered and dropped down.

"Go ahead," he said.

I stepped out of the box.

We were in a gymnasium, a large fully-equipped space containing the full panoply of modern equipment—treadmills, stairmasters, ellipticals, and a couple of bowflexes, along with a long row of colored dumbbells, circuit equipment, power cages, and a boxing ring.

Such a waste of space and money. You do not need any of that equipment to get yourself into ship-shape condition. In fact, I would argue, it hampers the effort. Your own body, used appropriately, is more than adequate. Most people haven't a clue. That cluelessness, however, keeps a lot of people employed. If things were sold based merely upon their necessity or usefulness, America's economy would collapse upon its already shaky foundations.

Television screens, too many to count, were the primary wall decorations.

A blonde model type, long hair flowing behind her like a TV commercial for shampoo, pounded peds on one of the treadmills while watching *Mad Men*. Two black men traded punches and insults in the boxing ring. Otherwise, the gym was empty.

I knew there were two other gyms and various spas scattered throughout the resort. This one was likely not open to the public.

The far side of the room held a wall of mirrors, and I watched myself watching myself between Art and Rex. They both had their eyes on me and I on them, or their reflections. They were sizing me up, trying to figure me out.

I put on my inscrutable face.

There were hallways leading away from the gym to my right and left.

"This where you guys buff your impressive physiques?"

They were a tough crowd. Rex touched me again on the elbow. "This way," he said and pointed to the hallway on the left. I eased my elbow away from his fingers and followed his direction.

Thus, we found ourselves in a small, square room with white walls, gray carpet, and no windows. A single desk with a glass top and swivel chair. Another swiveler was pushed into a back corner.

Three more men had gathered.

I was flattered to have drawn a crowd.

The two standing gentlemen had been produced by the same

cookie cutter responsible for the look of my escorts: biceps bulging, eyes flat, faces with expressions lacking *joie de vivre*.

The one sitting behind the desk had a prosperous gut, but his upper body was a tree trunk. His hands lay flat, motionless. A stapler, a basket of pens, papers stacked neatly, a pair of wire rims, an unwrapped sucker in a glass ashtray, a square plastic bottle of fancy water with bold calligraphy signaling its specialness.

Sitter was older than the other three men, perhaps mid-forties, but he too resembled a bull. Poe's job requirements were nothing if not utilitarian.

The other two men stood at opposite sides of the desk in erect military-style posture.

"Mr. Plank, why are you here?" the man at the desk asked, his index finger rising for a moment.

"Come to make my fortune."

The fist that took me by surprise shouldn't have. I buckled over, holding my gut. Rex had been aching to smack me since the moment we met.

I dropped to one knee, trying to catch a breath.

"Why are you here?" the older man repeated.

I winced, looked up. The men at the sides of the desk hadn't moved a muscle. Art was still a few steps behind me. I could sense Rex hovering above me, his fists clenched, eager.

"I need to talk to Poe," I managed.

"Not gonna happen," he responded.

"Shame," I said.

"Life," he offered.

"Tell me about it," I countered.

"We don't like you coming here and bothering our employees with questions about the boss." For the first time, his voice betrayed a tinge of malice.

I closed my eyes, visualizing the scene. Seconds passed.

I grabbed Rex's ankle and jerked it sharply back towards the center of his stance. As he started to fall, I socked him in the groin. He cried out, toppled over.

"Sucker punches irritate me," I said, jumping to my feet, my palms open at my side. "Just one of my pet peeves."

The two men at the desk hadn't had time to absorb and respond yet, but I sensed Art beginning to move behind me. Shifting my weight to my right foot for balance, I spun and slammed my left foot into his knee. He grunted. I broke his nose with my right elbow, and he collapsed.

I pivoted to face the others.

Nothing had changed in their positions, only the expressions on their faces. Since I like to move people emotionally, I was glad to see it.

"You're a dead man, Plank," desk man said, not bothering to raise his voice.

One of the standing men barked, "Fuckhead's in deep shit now."

"Sticks and stones," I retorted, relaxing my limbs, letting go of my mind, moving forward on the balls of my feet.

The Fuckhead Fulminator charged, fists first. I tripped him, and he fell at my feet. I spun, kicking him in the stomach, and he grabbed his solar plexus and gasped for air. A pair of hulking arms wrapped around my neck and tightened, lifting me up in the air. I dangled for a moment, then rocked my legs up and out and slammed my heels down on choker's feet. He screeched and let go. I whirled and caught him with a right hook. Somebody wrenched my legs out from beneath me. I fell and two bodies crashed down on top of me.

I grabbed an ear and twisted, poked an eye with my thumb. Screeching and howling in my ear. We rolled around on the floor for a few seconds, and then a voice broke through the chaos.

"Stop!"

Both men immediately rolled off me and knelt in a fair rendition of a yoga cat pose.

"Plank, are you alright?"

"Never been better. Things were just beginning to get interesting."

I looked up at Poe from my prone position on the floor.

"Did no one think to advise me that we had a visitor?"

A poignant silence filled the room. Somehow, his even tone and polite words achieved an eerie menace.

"Is it our policy to harass visitors to our place of business?"

Nothing.

"Please, leave us alone. At once."

The sound of bodies scrambling, shuffling, moving out of the room.

"Close the door behind you, Rex."

When we were alone, Poe murmured, "I'm sorry about that, Plank. They're good boys, all in all, but sometimes they get carried away and become overly diligent to their responsibilities."

I nodded. No way in hell Poe didn't know the moment I arrived and hadn't approved of everything that had happened until right now. I decided not to mention this fact to him, though. Couldn't see the point.

A rattler is a snake and always will be.

Poe offered me his hand. I took it and rose.

He was a short, thin man with a muscular build and a soft voice. He wore his black hair short and trim. He had cool blue eyes, a goatee, and an easy smile. He wore a long-sleeved white shirt and a black vest, his typical fare.

He looked like dirty money.

"I'm impressed. Those men you were dispensing a beating to are normally not to be taken lightly."

I shrugged. "*I have great faith in fools, my friends call it confidence.*"

Poe laughed. "Wonderful. I'd forgotten how amusing you can be." He clapped his hands together gleefully.

I'd quoted Edgar Allan before he did.

He shook his head, chuckled a little more. Delighted. "Come with me, won't you?"

He turned, and I followed him into an adjoining room.

POE'S MAN CAVE HAD ONE GLASS WALL WITH AN UNOBSTRUCTED view west toward the Golden Gate Bridge. Behind an antique walnut desk stood a tall bookshelf filled with volumes of Poe and other American Romantics—Hawthorne, Irving, Cooper.

A bust of Poe's namesake, looking harrowed and haunted, sat beside the books. Framed posters of old B-movies directed by Roger Corman and starring Vincent Price—*The Pit and the Pendulum, House of Usher, The Raven, Tales of Terror*—hung on the walls. On the desk was a miniature pendulum made out of dark wood.

All in all, the room of an academic, perhaps a bit obsessed by his subject. He was an Edgar Allan Poe freak with a surprising pedigree—a master's degree in English literature. His thesis had been on Edgar's influence on modern day horror writers. Only, Poe had left academia and his real name, Lawrence Fenderdale, far behind. How he'd gotten from Swarthmore to Pirate's Cove had to be a fascinating and horrible story in itself, worthy of the Edgar Allan treatment. I only knew a few anecdotes. No one seemed to know much of the tale except for Poe himself, and he hadn't written his memoirs yet.

He sat down behind his desk and bid me sit in a spit-shined black leather chair in front of it.

"Espresso?" he asked.

I nodded.

He pushed a button and said, "Two espressos please, Angelique."

He glanced out toward the sun-dappled waters, stretching out to the Gulf of the Farallones, and then looked back at me.

"A bit surprised to find you here without benefit of an appointment."

"It was a spur of the moment thing. I was out for a drive, mulling a problem over in my mind. All of a sudden, I wondered if perhaps you might be able to help me solve the thing. I just took a sharp left and found myself here."

"You are aware of my strong preference for advance notice."

It wasn't a question. Anybody who knew him knew, or better-had-damn- well-know, his preferences.

"Like I said, it was an impulse. Don't worry though. I won't be popping in on you all the time and—"

A tap on the opened door. A woman holding a silver tray. Poe motioned her in.

She was black, tall, big-boned. Her hair was short and frizzy, emphasizing her high cheekbones. She placed a demitasse cup and saucer with a cube of sugar wrapped in silver foil in front of me on the desk and then placed another in front of Poe.

I brought the cup to my nose and closed my eyes. I breathed in the earthy, aromatic smell and smiled. I took a sip and smiled again.

"Thank you, Angelique," I whispered.

She looked at me, nodded, and didn't smile with her beautiful full lips. She was intimidating. And sexy as hell. She left the room.

"She's a gem," Poe said. "A ninth dan black belt in Taekwondo and Hapkido. My toughest warrior. She could take any of the men out there that you beat down."

I figured her appearance was just to let me know that he had weapons upon weapons if need be. He needn't have bothered. I knew what I'd be facing if I ever presented a real threat. Poe himself was rumored to be proficient in the art of violence, particularly involving knives, although these days he generally eschewed force in favor of more genteel persuasions.

"Alright. Let's assume next time you'll make a proper appointment."

"Sure. What's your cell phone number?"

He gave me a look.

I shrugged. I knew I was supposed to make contact with one of his people on the street, who would then make contact with his contact, and so on and so forth, and then a few days later I'd get a note or a call with the meeting particulars. I didn't think Frankie should have to wait that long.

"So what is it that I can help you with today?"

I gulped down the rest of the espresso, smacked my lips, and said, "A little girl name of Frankie says you're a friend of hers."

"Frankie?"

"Yup. A few inches shy of five feet. Ponytail. Skateboard."

"Good kid," he said.

"Seems like it."

"I forgot. I did send her to see you, as I recall."

"That's why I'm surprised at the rough welcome."

"Boys misbehaving is all."

"Sure. How do you know Frankie?"

"Well..."

"Probably not the right question, is it?" I paused a moment for dramatic intensity. "It's Johnnie you know, isn't it?" Beautiful, twenty-two-year-old Johnnie.

"I have had the pleasure of getting to know both her and her sister."

"But Johnnie's the one that works for you."

Poe sighed. "She does not."

"What's your involvement then?"

He paused, pursed his lips. "I will not violate her privacy any more than I have to. She used to work in one of our clubs as a dancer. I came to know her. We were friends. She looked at me as a father figure or mentor. I was occasionally able to be of assistance to her."

Lord help Johnnie. I wanted to know more but figured he wouldn't tell me, so I got to the point. "What do you know about her disappearance?"

He took a sip of his espresso. The cup tinkled like a bell when he placed it back down on the saucer. "Unfortunately, not much. Just what poor Frankie told me. I guess Johnnie was in business for herself. Trading online. Sometimes selling things locally."

"You know about these guys she had a deal with? Blue Notes?"

He brushed his cheeks with his fingers, nodding. "The Blue Notes, yes. A Mission gang."

"What else?"

"That's why I sent her to you. You're the private investigator, no?"

Poe had informants all over the city, including the Mission, and he also had businesses in the district. He had to know more than he was telling me. It didn't make sense. Why would he involve me at all? Our previous encounters had been more than a tad gnarly, after all.

"I'm not a P.I."

"Same difference."

I shook my head, looked out the window. To my left, I could see several smaller boats a little ways away from the ocean cruiser moving toward the maw of the beast.

"So you can't help Frankie or your...friend, Johnnie?"

"I'd very much like to help. I've had a couple of acquaintances ask around, but nothing's turned up. She vanished and nobody seems to know why or where she's gone."

"Do you think she just took off and abandoned the little girl?"

"No. Not likely." He shook his head decisively.

"What about the Blue Notes?"

Poe stood up, walked to the window. With his back to me, he said, *"Hidden vices and perversions beneath the veneer of virtue."*

"Must be Edgar Allan."

A few seconds passed. With his back to me, he said, "Did you see my schooner out there? I'm going to have it refurbished, upgraded. Then I'm going to sail it around the Caribbean for a month. Me and..." He paused, clasped his hands in front of him. "Anyway, it's a great boat. I'm going to make it into a magnificent one."

I glanced out at the boat for a long moment, waiting.

Men with toys, just like boys.

"The Blue Notes started out around ten years ago as a group of recovering alcoholics and drug addicts, providing services. Soup kitchens, food banks, twelve step programs, even a dating service for addicts, or ex-addicts, I guess. But in the past several years, things have changed. The organization's been taken over. They still have some of the services, but they're a cover for drug dealing and other street crime—numbers, prostitution, extortion. Strictly local and small time, but pretty effective in their own way."

"Why do you let them operate?"

He turned to face me with a smile on his face. "You overestimate me. I can't control everything that goes on in this city and—"

"You could have fooled me." That was an exaggeration, but I knew he was susceptible to that kind of flattery. "Why haven't I heard of them?"

"They try to keep a low profile and stay out of the papers. Blue Notes is not their public name. The soup kitchens and food banks have generic names, like 'Mission OutReach' and the like." He returned to his chair and sat down, swiveling to face me. He formed his fingers into a pyramid. "As I stated, they're strictly small potatoes. But they sometimes resort to rather nasty practices. Best be careful if you pay a visit."

"The two guys Frankie mentioned, Scooter and Vince. You know anything about them?"

"A little. They're two of the gang leaders. The top gun is a Hispanic gentleman by the name of Caballo Negro, the Black Horse. He's a piece of work. Very full of himself, but smart and dangerous."

"Can you help me with them?"

Poe collapsed his fingers, folding them together. "I'm afraid that I cannot. I can only advise that you approach the group carefully and perhaps bring one of your associates who is not afraid of violence. I'd suggest Marsh."

"Frankie mentioned a car repair shop, Good & Plenty?"

He shrugged. "May be a place to start. Don't know where they're hanging out these days."

Something was wrong. Poe had to know more. He must have cared about Johnnie and Frankie since he referred her to me, but none of it made much sense. I guessed I'd probably have to come back here before I was through.

I got up, thanked him for the espresso, and left.

At the door, the black belt in Taekwondo was waiting for me. Just walking beside her provided a jolt to the old system. She moved like a dancer, a barely contained big cat. Our walk, side-by-side, felt like a sensuous dance, a stirring tango.

Maybe it was only me.

She stayed at my side, ignoring my stabs at chit-chat, until I reached the revolving carousel doors, freeing me from Pirate's Cove's clutch. I gave her my best smile and waved goodbye, but she didn't wave back.

CHAPTER 5

The *Sweet and Sour* is a beaut.

Eighty-five feet of fiberglass and carbon fiber, teak, and stainless steel. It has two jacuzzis, a pagoda, a game parlor, and a sky lounge.

Meiying kissed me on the cheek and said, "See, I tell you. Beautiful ladies."

I glanced around and shook my head, marveling. There were eight women on the main deck, each dressed in a variation of the long silky dress, each with elegantly coiffed hair pulled tight to magnificent skulls. All but one was Asian. All of the women were under thirty. I wondered what factory for porcelain perfection they'd been ordered from.

Dao did seem to have a knack for attracting young, pretty women. He liked to be surrounded by beauty in all its forms.

Meiying didn't seem to mind; she knew she had a firm hold on him.

There were also a half-dozen men present, most middle-aged —here again, all but one Asian. Dao knew that rich men were much more likely to show off their wealth when in the company of female pulchritude.

"Where's Dao?" I asked.

"Talking to Marsh downstairs. Take time. See Dao later. Here. Now. Be."

She caught the eye of an impossibly lovely Asian woman in a red dress and motioned for her to join us.

She slunk forward, poetry in motion. Twinkling black eyes, alabaster skin, hair as black as ink.

"Luli, this my friend, Max."

Luli extended her hand. Long, untamed fingers. Painted violet nails. I bowed, gently clasping her hand. "Absolute pleasure," I said.

She nodded, acknowledging the obvious. Luli possessed a subtle demureness tinged by a provocative animal aliveness in her movements.

Or something like that.

"Luli likes Murakami and Koons, Plank. Those are two of your favorites, too. I leave you alone to discuss." With that, she disappeared.

I'd never read Murakami. Koons' paintings left me cold.

FIFTEEN MINUTES LATER, I FOUND DAO AND MARSH CHAPIN huddled over green tea and blueprints in a corner of one of the staterooms, beneath a porthole that looked out on the Aquarium of the Bay.

They were an odd pair. I'd introduced them a couple of years ago when Marsh had stepped in to help Dao with a fellow yacht owner—a nasty racist, an unneighborly neighbor. Marsh had quickly "solved" the problem, sending the offending party scurrying to find a port far, far away from Dao. They'd got on famously since, sharing interests in Kabuki theater, traditional

Asian architecture, quantum physics, and the Boston Red Sox. To say nothing of commodities trading and the markets in general.

"Thanks for leaving me all alone with Meiying and her harem."

Dao looked up and smiled. "She thinks it's time you got married."

Dao was in his early sixties, short, balding, plump with a round face and intelligent eyes. He was whip-smart and knew more about money, finance, and economics than any three Ph.Ds in said fields.

"She's always thought that."

"You're not getting any younger." He stopped, laughed. "Her words, not mine."

Dao had been in this country since he was a little boy and had no accent, unlike Meiying, who'd not immigrated until she was almost thirty. Her family knew his family in Beijing, and she was sent over specifically to meet and marry Dao. He resisted until the moment he set eyes on her.

Marsh was leaning back in his chair, studying me.

"What?"

"He's right."

"What the hell are you talking about?"

"You're aren't getting any younger."

"You are?"

"I carry it better."

Actually, he did. He was a couple of years younger than me but looked like he was still in his twenties. He had golden hair and a rugged face with unblemished skin. His eyes were the color of burnished steel, appraising life and all those living it with a cool, hard matter-of-factness. His body wasn't overly muscled or bulky, but he was cut, lithe, and moved like a panther. He was a master of more esoteric martial arts than I had names for. He'd trained me, adding significantly to my arsenal of basic but pretty effective moves.

He'd been with Special Forces during part of the Afghanistan war and, I think, was still available for "consultations." He didn't ever talk about it, but I'd seen his "expertise," and it was scary.

I didn't like to be around at those times when he put his training into practice. I'm not prone to nightmares, but I didn't want to risk it.

"I don't see you and Tom walking down the aisle."

"Please."

Marsh was never on board with the rush to have gay marriage sanctioned. He was a rogue, through and through, and had no interest in rules and regulations, or in any government or church sanction about how to live.

"Anyway, Tom left."

"You mean you kicked him out." Tom was head over heels. They'd been together almost a year, the longest relationship of Marsh's life.

"It was time."

I nodded. I liked Tom but knew it probably wasn't going to last. Marsh was and always would be a loner.

"We need to talk."

Marsh studied my face, then dipped his chin.

I walked closer to their table. "Blueprints?"

"Marsh has a good idea for a small Kabuki theater here on the Wharf. The Fondue Fanatic is looking for a buyer. Good price. No other Kabuki in the whole city."

"Where will you get the performers?"

"No problem. Here. There. Everywhere," Dao said.

I didn't know a thing about Kabuki, who performed, or who was interested in seeing it.

"What about tonight? Are you going to pitch soon?"

"Pitch. I do not pitch," Dao said, frowning. "I offer opportunities."

"Sorry, I can't stay. I'm not your target audience anyway. I actually still buy my own groceries."

"Meiying will be upset if you do not make a date with one of the ladies."

"I'll see what I can do on my way out." I turned back to Marsh. "Can you meet me on the pier in ten minutes?"

He nodded.

"Go upstairs first and have some gunpowder chicken and hoisin, please, Plank."

"I will definitely do that." My mouth was already watering in anticipation.

"Cribbage?" Dao asked.

"Same old. Tomorrow. Rusty Root at 5."

Dao nodded and turned back to the blueprints.

MARSH AND I STOOD UNDER THE SHADOW OF THE AWNING OF THE Aquarium of the Bay. The three-quarter moon blazed in the night sky. The water lapped the edges of the pier, a big cat slurping.

"You ever hear of an organization called the Blue Notes?"

"Like the club in New York?"

"More like the gang in the Mission."

"Can't say that I've had the pleasure."

"It seems not many people, outside of Poe and the cops, have."

"Newspapers aren't what they used to be. Poe, you say?"

I nodded and told him about Frankie and my meeting with Poe and the little he'd told me about the Blue Notes.

"I know Angelique. Best watch your p's and q's around her."

"How do you know her?"

Marsh looked away for a moment, deflecting the question. "So how is the little girl paying you?"

"In doubloons."

Marsh was under the impression that I had a bit too much

Don Quixote in me, especially when it came to women of any age. He'd been the one who commissioned my stained-glass front door with its Knights of the Roundtable theme.

"You going to visit some of these Blue Notes?"

"Looks like it."

"There's a great dive, Mamasita's, off Market and 16th. *Tacos al Carbon* to trade your first kid for."

"Tomorrow at 11 a.m.?"

Marsh nodded and turned away.

"Too bad about Tom and you," I called out.

His shoulders rose and fell, as he offered a dismissive wave of his hand.

CHAPTER 6

I left Marsh in the driver's seat of his Aston Martin across the street from Good & Plenty Repairs on 25th and Sanchez.

The corrugated metal door was rolled down tight, despite the fact that it was 1:30 p.m. The storefront had a decrepit Spanish tile roof with a weathered white brick facing. Two adjoining windows were covered by white poster paper and secured with iron bars.

We'd lingered at Mamasita's, and I'd probably had one too many *Negro Modelos* and, for sure, one more habanero-laced taco than I needed.

I burped and glanced back across the street. Marsh nodded. The Aston Martin was neon yellow. A crowd of teenagers was already gathering around it.

Kitty corner to the body shop was a tiny grocery, Amash Produce. I wandered in, felt up a couple of green bananas and an orange, and piled them all together in a bag.

A weigh scale sat next to the cash register, and I plopped the bag on top of it. A man from somewhere in the Levant part of the world, who had to be at least eighty—white-haired, his skin a network of brown wrinkles folded over upon themselves—eyed the scale, removed the bag, and said, "$3.55."

I paid him, turned away, paused, turned back.

"Do you know when the garage next door will be open?"

He frowned, shook his head, lifted his hands. "Who knows, mister. Kids don't know how to run a business. How they keep it open?" He glanced out nervously toward the front door. "I do not bring my car there, mister. If I am you, I listen."

"So you know the owners?"

"Nobody here knows them. Really, sir. Punks. One or another of these hoodlums comes in here sometimes, usually for candy or to steal. This one, Marley, gives me very hard time. He just takes. He never pays." The old man reached under the counter and came back up with a small revolver in his hand. "I think sometimes," he muttered, staring at the piece, then sighed. "But I'm an old man. Jalil just wants to be left alone."

He lowered the gun back into its slot beneath the register.

"One boy is nice. Not like the others. But, like the others, he has no father. His mother, who I have met, a nice woman, but too much for her. She always works. Her son is Vince. Vince is good boy, mainly. He needs friends, and so he has these punks for friends. I have talk to him. So have police. They are often here. But he is young, and he does not listen." Jalil shook his head, his jowls sagging, his eyes pooling with the ravages of a thousand years living at the margins.

"So they don't keep regular hours? They might not open again today?"

He glanced again at the door as if expecting trouble and bad luck to walk in, arm in arm, at any moment. "I cannot say more. Take your business elsewhere. Thank you."

He handed me my bag of produce with a trembling hand.

I PRESSED A ROUND BLACK RINGER NEXT TO THE GARAGE'S DOOR AND waited. After a long pause, I hit it again and didn't let go. The annoying, high-pitched buzz kicked up a racket inside.

From the corner of the building, a face appeared above a crumbling brick fence. "What the fuck you want?"

"Car needs work." I pointed across the street to the Aston Martin.

The boy's eyes widened. "You're shitting me?"

"The engine light came on. It's overheating. We need somebody to look at it right away."

He couldn't take his eyes off the car. Marsh waved at him. "Hold on a minute." He disappeared.

A minute later, the accordion doors creaked upward and three young men stood in front of me.

Jalil had hit the nail on the head. If you looked in a picture dictionary under the word "punk," you couldn't have done better than to depict these three fine, youthful specimens.

There was hardly an inch of skin on any of them that hadn't been tattooed or pierced. Personally, I think tattoos are a scourge, an insult to a perfectly fine canvas. I don't like 'em, never did, never will. But that's a personal thing. I know some really nice people who have a liking for indelible ink. And this is America after all, home of the brave and the witless.

But these boys had jumped the shark vis-a-vis body decoration, and, even worse, there didn't seem to be an ounce of youthful lightness or optimism in their faces. It was all pose and sneer, challenge and defiance.

I doubted they had much walk-in business.

The Asian boy stepped forward. "I'm Louie," he said finally. "These my homies, Jason and Tart."

I extended my hand. "I'm Max."

Louie looked at it as if it had just arrived from Venus.

"Gentlemen, a pleasure," I said. "Are you the mechanics?"

Tart grinned, looked nervously at Louie. Jason farted. Louie kept a straight face. "Yeah. We work on cars all the time."

"Is the owner here?"

"Nope."

"Is that Scooter?"

"Yeah. Scooter. He's not here. I'm his brother," Louie said.

"I see," I said. "Okay." I waved my hand out towards the Aston. "My friend's car has a problem. The engine light is on. It appears to be overheating. We're late for an appointment. Can you help?"

Louie, with two nose rings and a dragon tattoo crawling from his pinky finger to his Adam's apple, tossed his smoldering cigarette to the ground. "Whoah. That's some ride, buddy. Yeah. We can take a look at it for ya."

"You're lifesavers."

I motioned to Marsh. The Aston purred to life and inched forward.

MARSH STROLLED NEXT DOOR TO AMASH AND PICKED UP A Hershey bar and a milk. While he ate, we loitered near a lamp post a half-block from where the boys gathered around the Aston.

"So what's the plan?" Marsh asked, offering me a square of chocolate.

I declined. "I'm in an improvisational mood today. We lit a match, now let's wait and see." I paused, glanced back at the garage. Tart was smoking a cigarette, standing watch, the occasional sideward glance our way, while the other two boys stayed under the hood. "You messed with the spark plugs?"

Marsh winced, took a gulp from his pint of milk. "It truly pained me to violate her. I also loosened the gas cap. Should be an easy fix for the boys."

Marsh hardly ever took "her" out of his garage. We figured the

$175,000 car would present maximum temptation to our mechanics.

"I have a subtle feeling they're going to complicate matters." I looked back again. Tart stubbed out his cigarette, gave me what could have been a smile or a sneer, and rejoined the boys inside.

We decided to let them have a little time to themselves, time to let their true natures percolate, and walked around the block. We encountered a homeless man who beseeched us for cash. Marsh offered him the second half of his chocolate bar. The man cursed him and stumbled away. The neighborhood had a lot of yipping dogs and overturned garbage cans.

Back at the garage, we found the accordion door once again slammed shut. Marsh peered over the brick fencing. "Can't see much. A narrow alley with cracked concrete and weeds. It angles away behind the garage."

"Let's go over," I said.

We scaled the five-foot wall and dropped down onto the other side.

"I fear we misjudged the mendacity of the youngsters, but they had better not hurt a hair on her head," he said, and I felt a chill run through me at the tenor of Marsh's voice. I hoped the boys weren't as dumb as they looked.

At the end of the alley, we found an open door leading back into the garage. Inside, the Aston Martin rested quietly in the center of the room. In a tight corner beneath a hanging ring of tires, the boys were playing poker on a makeshift table, four tires stacked and topped with a piece of metal siding.

"Louie," I called out.

"Hey," he said, not bothering to look at me, a cigarette dangling from his lips. He flipped his hand—three jacks—laughed, and raked in a bunch of change and a few bills.

"Fuckheads," he said. "Your tell's too easy, Tart. Like taking candy from a monkey."

"A baby," Tart barked.

"Baby. Monkey. Dumb is dumb." Louie ground out his cigarette on the metal. "Ride's ready," he continued. "No big deal. Spark plug. You left your gas cap loose, too. Everything should be copafuckingcetic."

I stood there for a moment trying to improvise. And it wasn't just Louie's surprising familiarity with the word *copacetic* that threw me.

Finally, I came up with, "How much do we owe you?"

He slashed the air with his hand dismissively.

Had I fallen into an alternate universe where juvenile delinquents had a different, more Disney-esque mode of being?

"For your time," I tried.

"Just tell your rich friends to bring their cars here. We'll give 'em a deal. Start getting Astons and Ferraris and Mercedes in here 'stead of the usual shitty old rides, we're going to be sittin' in shit heaven. Keys in the visor. Open sesame, Tart."

He cursed, threw his cards down on the table. "You're a lucky a-hole, Louie."

"Luck's got nuthin' ta do with it, T. Just figurin' out the stupid."

Tart hit a red button, and the folding entrance to the garage stuttered open.

I started toward the car, stopped. "Are you three the primary mechanics?"

Louie frowned.

"I just...I want to recommend you and wanted to make sure that—"

"Answer to your question is yeah. Lately. Scooter doesn't have much time for the business and—"

Tart snorted. Jason laughed.

Louie ignored them. "...and so I'm kinda in charge at this point. Tell 'em Louie will take good care of 'em."

CHAPTER 7

"Interesting."

"I don't get it."

"Youth can be a perplexing time."

"Does anything about that make sense to you?"

Marsh turned on the radio, and Vivaldi's violins sang rapturously through the Aston's spectacular speakers. "Looks like the ones we met may not be directly involved in funny business. Probably Scooter and the Blue Notes used this as a front of some sort, or he started it legit and lost interest. Maybe he's turned it over to his younger, more industrious brother."

I mulled that over. Based upon Tart and Jason's reaction to Louie's comment about his brother not having time for the business, it was pretty clear the boys did know what Scooter was up to. If and why they were not involved was less clear. Maybe Scooter was trying to keep his younger brother on the straight and narrow? Seemed like a subplot of a hackneyed TV crime show, but clichés sometimes operate quite nicely in the real world.

"Where to?" Marsh asked as we pulled away from the curb.

STRAY CAT BLUES 55

I thought for a moment about my boat, my hammock on the back deck, a cool drink in my hand, the sound of the water gently lapping the hull, and sighed. I made a sudden decision and told Marsh where to go.

FROM FRANKIE'S VIVID DESCRIPTION, I DIDN'T THINK IT'D BE TOUGH to find where she lived, and it wasn't.

The scarecrow wasn't exactly a dead ringer for Ray Bolger in the *Wizard of Oz*. It was four pieces of plywood painted black, covered by a black velvet dress and a blonde wig over a painted Mardi Gras mask. The birds pecking away at the vegetable garden beneath were unimpressed.

The chicken weather vane on the roof was a work of art—a funky melding of metal and copper piping configured to resemble a red rooster crowing at the heavens.

I left Marsh to his Vivaldi in the Aston and strolled around to the side of the house where a narrow concrete stairwell angled and disappeared into a covered porch. I scaled the stairs and found myself in the midst of a tropical jungle. Palms and orchids and snapdragons, long flowering vines in pastel colors filled up virtually every inch of the small wood-framed porch's terra cotta floors. Insects buzzed and flitted about the deep, wet depths of the foliage. A strong vanilla scent with a hint of grape filled the air, along with something else more pungent. A weedy scent. I thought immediately of pot, but couldn't glimpse any, although there was so much dense greenery that it could have been buried there somewhere. With marijuana legalized for medical use, there were more than a few home farmers in the city now, growing the stuff to treat every and any manner of illness, real or imagined.

I tiptoed around the assorted pots and planters and tapped three times on a door that was a tapestry of memories from the psychedelic sixties: Day-Glo colors, guitars, flower children, and peace symbols, drawn with childlike simplicity.

As I looked around me, a bit overwhelmed by the sights and sounds and smells, a stirring, a step from inside reached my ears.

A moment later, the door creaked open a few inches until it was stopped by a latched gold chain. A single blue eye, framed by a high forehead and dirty blonde hair, peeked out at me.

"Hello. Max Plank. Looking for Frankie."

The door closed. A moment passed. The door opened.

No surprise. She was a throwback to a more innocent time of incense, free love, rock music when it mattered, and girls dressed in their summer clothes. Her natural cloth fiber neck-to-ankle dress hung on her like it was still on a wire hanger in a closet.

"Frankie lives here?" I asked.

"Wait," she said, a perplexed smile on her lips. "Wait..."

I did that.

"...it's only..." Her lovely green eyes were a little spacey. The pungent smell on the porch intensified momentarily, or maybe it was just my sensory imagination, adding up two plus two.

"...yes. I think. No. C'mon, Mr.?"

"Plank. Max."

"Max." Her weak smile broadened. "I like that. Max. Such a strong name for a man." Her eyes took me in, running the length and breadth of me. "Very strong. My name is Maggie, Max. C'mon."

She stepped back. I ambled in.

WE SAT ON BEAN BAG CHAIRS—MINE RUBY RED, HERS A VIOLENT shade of pink—in a front room that overlooked Church Street and Mission Dolores Park.

Outside it was late afternoon and the fog had rolled in, a ghostly mist like a warning of worse things to come. The only lights inside were the candles surrounding us on all sides. Incense filled the air with a stomach-turning sweetness.

"Green tea?"

"No, thank you. I understand that Frankie lives here and that you are her landlord."

She recoiled as if I'd slapped her. "I hate that word. It's so...legal...so capitalist. As if because we happen to be caretakers of this property that we are the oppressive lords over it and any who live here."

Such a fresh perspective.

"So you don't own it? You're only taking care of the house?"

"I didn't mean that. The home has been in Leonard's family for several generations, so technically we do own it. It's just that language, I mean, it's so important, isn't it? Language can fool us...that's what Leonard always says."

I nodded. The expression on her face was a mix of concern and embarrassment. I thought perhaps it wasn't only language that fooled or confused her.

"Is Frankie here?"

"That's what I was trying to remember..."

"Whether she's here or not?"

"No. No. You, Max. Frankie told me about you."

I nodded again.

She rubbed the back of her hand across her forehead in a gesture that reminded me of Vivien Leigh as Blanche DuBois in *A Streetcar Named Desire*. She scratched her head, wrinkled her nose, blinked repeatedly. "I'm remembering now." She looked up at me, and her eyes widened in sudden surprise. "You're a private investigator? You're trying to help Frankie?"

"I'm not a private investigator, but—" I was wasting my time trying to explain to her the intricacies of what I was and how I operated. "I am trying to help her find her sister."

Maggie was staring intently at a grouping of large candles

dripping copious amounts of wax on the pockmarked fireplace mantle. Without looking at me, she said, "I can't say that I approve of most law enforcement practices...although I imagine that they are sometimes a necessary evil." She glanced at me for a brief moment, then her eyes searched a corner of the room. "But I am glad that someone is helping that poor little girl. It's just awful. Her parents dying and now her sister, her protector, vanished into thin air."

"Do you know what happened to her parents?"

Her eyes flared to life. "I gather that her father was a ne'er-do-well of some sort who left when Johnnie was a teenager, right after Frankie was born. Her mother died a few years back. Cancer. Dragged on for a while. Must have been just awful." Maggie's voice had suddenly become strangely animated, her face twitching, her fingers making jerky movements. My mind was stuck on ne'er-do-well—it seemed an archaic expression coming out of her mouth.

"Is there anything that was going on here about the time that Johnnie disappeared?" I tried.

She sat up straighter. Her eyes narrowed, and she frowned again. "What...can you mean?"

"I was just wondering if there was anything unusual that you happened to notice about Johnnie or her behavior? Anything that, looking back now, you think might seem a bit odd or funny. Something, anything, that might have some link to her disappearance. Any strangers or suspicious people hanging about?"

Her body relaxed. I wasn't accusing her of anything. "I don't know. I guess not. Can't remember anything special. Leonard and I didn't see the girls a lot. We had them for dinner once, but that was almost a year ago. Leonard had a lot of sympathy for the girls' situation. That's why he agreed to take them in." She nodded her chin up and down, agreeing with herself.

"So you were doing them a favor?"

"Sure...I mean how many people are going to rent to a young woman like Johnnie, with no real means of support, and a little girl?"

"You weren't worried they wouldn't be able to make rent?"

"I was. But Leonard is an old softie with a heart of gold and—"

"Did I hear my name?"

A man appeared off a hallway beside the front room. I guessed his age at none-too-shy of a half century, while Maggie was still mired in her confused twenties.

He was short, shorter than Maggie's roughly five-foot-eight, with a stout body. He had red hair tied back in a ponytail and gold wire rims. His nose was pointy, his eyes dark brown. He wore a blue stitched Pendleton over faded jeans and scuffed black boots.

Maggie seemed surprised. Taken off balance. In a voice that was a bit sweeter and higher than the one she was using with me, she said, "Honey pie, I thought you were napping."

"Was. Aren't now." His gaze fixed on me. "And you must be..."

"Max Plank. Dropped by to see Frankie. As I was telling Maggie here, I'm trying to look into the matter of her missing sister."

Leonard took a seat on the floor next to Maggie's chair.

"What have I missed?"

"Nothing, really. Mr. Plank here was just..."

"I was just asking if either of you had noticed anything strange or unusual before or anywhere around the time Johnnie disappeared. Any new or old faces visiting or hanging around. Any people or cars loitering in front of the house. Any behavior by Johnnie, or even Frankie, that might indicate a problem or stress. Anything at all. Even if it might seem small or silly, you never know about what might link to a situation like this."

"And what kind of situation do you think we have here?" Leonard's tone was not altogether friendly.

"Hard to say. I'm just gathering information, and this is the first logical place to look."

"So you don't think that Johnnie just got overwhelmed with raising a little girl and decided to disappear?"

"I can't say. But from what Frankie and others say, it doesn't seem likely."

"I don't think so either. Johnnie was devoted to her sister," Leonard said as if I'd just passed a short quiz.

"So, back to circumstances around her disappearance. Anything you can tell me?"

"I don't know what Maggie here said—"

"Nothing. Nothing Len, really," Maggie said quickly, her fingers clenching on her kneecaps.

"Then I have to echo my woman. I can't think of anything in particular. We haven't seen much of either girl lately. Just one of those things. Frankie came up every now and then when Johnnie was gone and she was lonely. Johnnie had to be out a lot, trying to make ends meet and so, even at night, sadly, the girl was on her own."

"Do you know much about how Johnnie earned money? I understand she had an online business, but Frankie didn't really understand the details. I'd like to talk to any associates she had, or customers even, but I'd have to locate them first."

"'Fraid not. I know she did some things on the Internet. She'd buy things, art and stuff, and then resell it. I don't know how it all worked. She did make some money. Most times, the rent was on time. I wouldn't get too bent out of shape when it was a few days late. I understood she was doing the best that she could." Leonard stared at his feet in the big black boots, lifting them up high, then slowly lowering them back down to the floor.

I had the urge to ask what the two of them did to make their living.

Outside on the street, a car horn blared and somebody

shouted, then cursed. The fog dimming the window light made me feel melancholy. Sitting with Leonard and Maggie didn't help. I had the distinct feeling that they were not telling me the truth, the whole truth, and nothing but the truth so help them, Jesus.

"So you don't know any of their friends or acquaintances? No one whose name you could give me?"

"Not a soul. Never saw a single person visit. She never had any kind of get-together or party that we're aware of."

I looked at Maggie, whose body language and expression had changed significantly since her man entered the room. Like someone had turned her dimmer down to low. The vacant look she'd greeted me with had returned and she didn't seem to be listening to the conversation.

There was a knock at the porch door, and Maggie jumped to her feet. She opened it to a young couple. The boy, barely past the age of consent, wore a leather jacket and had a half-finished cigarette dangling from his lips. He was trying to look bored beyond belief. The girl with him was a waif in every sense of the word. She leaned against him, her arm clutching his waist. She was shaved bald with a narrow mohawk. Her eyes flitted about the room searching for purchase.

Nobody said a word. Maggie led them down the hallway to the back of the house.

"Anything else we can do for you?" Leonard said, his tone suddenly impatient.

"Do you know where Frankie is right now?"

"Not a clue."

"Okay." I stood up. "Thanks for your time."

Leonard rose. I did the same and headed for the door.

"If I think of anything that might help, how can I contact you?"

I gave him my card. A simple white slip containing nothing but my name and cell phone number in mild black letters. He stared at it for a moment and nodded.

"I'll let myself out."

"Good luck, Plank. That little girl needs some."

When I slid back into the plush comfort of the Aston's passenger seat, Marsh had his eyes closed to Mozart's *Don Giovanni*.

"A better use of time than our previous encounter, I trust."

I shrugged. My mind was already working on the information Maggie and Leonard provided. They were a trip, to speak in their parlance. There was nothing too unusual about them, at least not measured by San Francisco standards. But, even before the young desperate couple showed up at their door, I'd had an uneasy feeling, something that I couldn't exactly put my finger on. One thing I was sure of was that the two of them weren't merely good Samaritans. I couldn't tell if they cared a lick about Frankie.

"Time to go home?" Marsh asked.

I glanced at my cell phone. I was late for Dao. "The Rusty Root, my good man." I punched in Dao's number to tell him I was going to be a bit tardy.

Marsh started up the Aston and frowned. "I guess I've got to go face the music. Tom's waiting for me at home. He broke in...using his key, which I told him to return. He says he won't leave until we talk."

"Probably not a bad idea, Marsh. Communication is the key to relationship success. I do think you owe him a little closure."

"Closure," Marsh snarled, shaking his head at the ridiculousness of the concept while flooring the gas pedal.

CHAPTER 8

I was in danger of being double-skunked.

"Damn it, Dao." He was an expert player and nothing got past him, but tonight he was pegging at a supernatural clip.

"Study the past if you would divine the future," Dao mumbled as he dropped a seven on my eight, adding another peg. "Fifteen-two."

He liked to quote Confucius to irk me.

Dao has been playing cribbage since he was a toddler, and he taught me a couple of years ago. We have a weekly game, or actually series of games, whatever number we can fit in in a couple of hours at the Root.

Cribbage is a relatively simple and straightforward game, but like most simple things that are worth your time, it has endless permutations in the play and, in particular, the scoring, which borders on the insane. I'm still discovering the occasional new way to score a point or peg. In other words, we encounter a new situation where Dao informs me that an incomprehensible point he's about to take is legit.

I've never checked with any official Cribbage bible. I take his word for it, although not without making sure to add the appropriate grumbling regarding the unfairness of the game and the world.

"So how'd you do on your opportunity party the other night?"

"Excellent. You should consider a small investment."

If I had money to spare, which I rarely do, I might. But only because it's Dao. My money is always spoken for, usually before I earn it. I trust Dao and know he'd, without doubt, do well by me. But I don't believe in investing or saving for the future or mutual funds or insurance or 401Ks, or any other reasonable long term strategy, no matter how safe.

There is no insurance policy in the world that will make me feel more secure.

I'm not a spendthrift. In fact, I rarely shop for anything, online or off. My boat has needs, and I take care of them. Otherwise, I spend only on necessities, the women in my life being part and parcel.

Life is a risk. Tomorrow may never come. I hold to those philosophies, but for good and ill, I also have an innate contrariness. If most everybody agrees something is true, there has to be something false or wrong about it.

"I'll think about it, Dao."

"No, you won't. It's okay, Max. I understand." And he did. That's why I liked spending time with him. Meiying was another matter. She couldn't help herself, but I loved her, too, and she had only my best interests at heart, albeit filtered through a different culture and consciousness.

"And you did not call the lovely Luli either, my friend. Meiying is disappointed."

"I wanted to read at least one Murakami novel first," I said. I'd considered Luli, and every time I considered her, my pulse quickened. I'd so far resisted the temptation. Besides, Alexandra was in town, and Luli's considerable charms paled in comparison.

Dao laughed and shook his head.

"You are a funny man, Plank. Very funny."

That's me. A laugh riot.

I glanced back down at my overturned cards and said, "Fifteen-two, four, six, eight and two is ten." I moved my peg to within four holes of the double-skunk line. I wasn't going to win, but perhaps I could still avoid total Cribbage humiliation.

"Marsh told me you went to see Poe."

I looked at the pathetic cards in my hand and hoping that Dao would play something that would allow me to peg over that skunk line before he counted out of the game. "I did."

"At his casino?"

"It was awe-inspiring."

"I've only seen pictures in the paper. It looks like a dangerous sea creature."

"That it does and is."

"Gambling is a waste of money and time."

"Good spot to meet women, though."

"Depends on what kind of women you like to meet."

"You'd be surprised. Some fine ladies love the excitement of pulling the handle on a slot machine and watching the blur of potential money clarify before their eyes. Wouldn't be surprised if Meiying was one of those." I was ribbing him now.

He frowned, his eyes flitting to one side. He nodded. "Perhaps."

He was a smart man, a practical man, a man with keen insight into human behavior. He'd told me before that his wife was the mystery at the heart of his life.

I put down my final card, a six and, of course, Dao topped it with a nine and took two points on the peg. He had first count and more than enough to go out.

I was left a slot shy of the double-skunk line.

Dao said, "Good game."

"No, it wasn't."

"Humility is good for the soul, Max." He smiled without a trace of ridicule or malice.

"Namaste," I said, placing my hands into a prayer position and bowing my head.

Dao laughed.

IN THE MIDDLE OF THE NEXT GAME, WITH ME ONCE AGAIN TRAILING badly, Bo Fiddler wandered over and pulled up a chair. He was wearing his work uniform—a white linen shirt over a pair of dark clean jeans secured by a leather belt with a large gold buckle depicting a Remington-esque character in action, a cowboy with a lasso on a steed.

"How goes it?" He took a bite of a green apple, the crunch and crackle and sweet smell wafting over the table. "Looks like Custer's Last Stand, Plank. Have you won a game yet?"

I glared at him. This was our fifth game of the night.

"Did you meet with my landlord?" he said, examining the cratered apple introspectively.

Dao topped my three with a five, bringing the hand to a neat thirty-one close and taking an additional five points. I was only going to be single-skunked in this game.

As Dao shuffled, I said, "We had an impactful meeting." I filled in the necessary details.

"I admire your chutzpah, pal. Doesn't speak well for your long-term survival prospects, but old age is overrated anyhow."

"If I am going to help Frankie, I couldn't wait. That's all there was to that."

Bo took another bite out of his apple and smiled. "Sure, buddy."

"Could you do me a favor?" I asked, picking up my cards with that ridiculous little feeling of rising hope that never seems to die. I cursed, dropping the cards back down to the table.

Shaking my head in disgust, wondering what I'd done to offend the prickly Gods of Cribbage, I explained what I wanted Bo to do.

"You're kidding," Bo said.

"No," I said, and reluctantly picked up the cards that all but guaranteed my further demise.

"Damn." Bo took another bite of the apple and mumbled around the crumbling core, "Balls and chutzpah, Plank. Balls and chutzpah."

As we were finishing up a platter of steamed cajun potstickers and green tea, Meiying arrived.

She put her hand on Dao's shoulder, and he reached up and placed his on top of hers. She looked at me expectantly and said, "Your little girl came by see you again today."

"She did?"

"I take her to your boat but..." Meiying shrugged.

"What time?" Marsh had picked me up around 10 a.m.

"Lunch time."

"She left?"

"I fed her lunch. Moo shu and Hoisin wraps. Juice. Coconut ice cream. I let her watch TV, *Arrow* on Netflix. Then we go back to your boat but..." She shrugged her shoulders again as if to indicate that the inscrutable comings and goings of Max Plank were incomprehensible to women and children alike.

"And?" I said.

"Finally she go."

"Did she say anything about why she wanted to see me?"

Meiying pursed her lips and moved her hand to Dao's neck. Her fingers began to gently massage him there, and his eyes lost a touch of their focus.

"She not say too much. Just that she need to speak with Mr. Plank."

"What time was it that she left?"

"Maybe four."

I'd left her house a little after 3:30 p.m., so even if she'd gone straight there, I would have missed her.

"I think Frankie have trouble that no little girl should have."

I locked eyes with hers and nodded.

"Can Dao and Meiying help?"

"I don't know...next time she shows up and I'm not here, call my cell phone."

I should have given the kid my cell number, but I'm not in the habit of sharing it with anybody but those closest to me. And, even then, I do it grudgingly. I'm not exactly the poster boy for social connectivity.

"You not answer your cell phone most of time."

That was true. I often didn't bother to carry it.

"You help Frankie, Max. She is good girl. She wash lunch dish. She thank me three times for letting her on boat. But I can see on her face the pain. She try to be tough. Help her."

I nodded. So far the case had stayed closed tight to my efforts to pry it open just a bit. Whatever it was trapped inside was burrowed deep, like some tenacious tapeworm resistant to the light of day. I was probably going to have to take more extreme action to coax it to the surface.

CHAPTER 9

Alexandra Stone sat at a corner table of Bertolucci's, sipping amber liquid from a cocktail glass, looking perfectly at ease and comfortable in her own skin.

She wore an unpretentious but lovely purple dress that couldn't hide the lushness of her upper body. The tapering curves of her legs from knees to ankles were bare for all to admire.

She smiled when she saw me, and I smiled back. It had been almost six weeks since I'd seen her, and I'd missed that smile more than I realized.

She stood and hugged me, and I echoed the favor. Pulling back, she examined my face. "Max," she said, in a voice that lit a fuse in my toes that ran up the length of my spine. She gave me a quick, firm kiss on the lips, and then sat back down.

"You look...well like you. And here's looking at you, kid," I joked, but I couldn't take my eyes off of her.

"I've missed you," she murmured.

We'd only talked once, briefly, while she was gone. I guess neither one of us much liked spending time on the phone.

The waiter dropped by, and I ordered a gin martini and a plate of calamari.

"I thought you'd finally given up on me."

She gave me a wry look. "Just busy. A story that's led me from Bangkok to Dubai to San Francisco, to mention but three ports of call."

"What's it all about?"

"It's confusing." She looked over my shoulder for a moment, gathering her thoughts. "I thought I was investigating a new currency trading scheme, but it's led me to something else, I think. It's still a little early, and I have lots more digging to do, although I have my doubts that I can ever link things up and find the direct connections."

"You know how investigative work works, Alex. If it's anything like mine, you just chip away slowly and maybe, if you're lucky, after a while some of the grit and gristle will wear off and you can get a peek at the truth."

"I know. But I'm a little queasy about this one. I'm almost afraid to dig down deeper. It involves the slave trade. Really yucky stuff."

Alexandra was an investigative reporter, and sometimes photographer, for *The Independent*, one of Great Britain's best magazines. It was tough and anti-establishment and uncompromising in its principles and goals. Just like her.

"I'll tell you more later if you want. How about you? Have you been taking it easy and staying away from work and the world like you wanted to?"

"Sort of." I wanted to tell her about the case and Frankie, but I didn't want to do it right then and there. Her scent, a subtle hint of soap and sweet berries and Alex herself, wafted over me and I drank it in. I took her all in—her overwhelming womanliness and life force. She had a hint of a smile on her face, and there was more than a hint of tenderness for me in her eyes. I didn't want to talk about schemes and slaves and children lost in the world.

I wanted her naked and in my arms.

"Max?"

I was lying in my bed with the moonlight filtering jagged slivers of light across my body through a small port window. The bed sheets were tangled around me, the comforter tossed on the floor. Alex was in my nose, my head, my bruised-good lips.

I realized I'd dozed off for a little while. When I looked up, I spotted her on the other side of the boat. She was at my open front door, staring out at the bay. She was naked, and looking at her I reacted, the ache in my groin returning again, despite our recent couplings.

"Come back to bed. I need you."

She turned around and faced me. "C'mon, Max."

Her heavy breasts swayed slightly, and my already stimulated imagination took a flight of fancy, making things harder on me.

"Here." I moved on my side, making room for her. "Come snuggle."

She gave me a look.

"I promise to be a good boy."

"You're no fun," she murmured sexily, and ambled to the bed with swinging hips that any church worth its salt would have declared sinful—and any state wanting civilized order, downright illegal.

She cozied up to me, letting me wrap my arms back around her while she nestled her soft bottom up against the center of my body.

Between our first and second bout of sexual intimacy, I'd told her all about Frankie and Johnnie, and Poe, and Maggie and Leonard, and the boys at the garage. She'd listened with her usual intensity and was about to ask a question when I silenced her with a long kiss, which led to another, and another, until the world and its troubles vanished for us.

Now she came back to it. "The little girl, Frankie. She's living all alone now?"

"Yes. She's in Maggie and Leonard's downstairs apartment."

"Will they look out for her?"

"Maggie maybe, but she's got problems of her own, including Leonard."

"A twelve-year-old shouldn't be living all by herself. Who's going to—"

"She's a tough kid. She's had to grow up quickly. I think she's capable of taking care of herself for a little while."

"What about money? Food? The basics?"

"She offered me money to find her sister. A few hundred bucks or so. I'm sure that's enough to keep her stomach full for a while."

"You didn't take any money from her, did you?"

"Uh-uh."

"Good boy." She emphasized this by moving her bottom up and down against me a couple of times. I was a good boy and I deserved it.

"But I still think you're going to have to contact somebody soon about her care if you don't find her sister."

"I already mentioned that to her, but she was aghast at the thought."

I told her about how Johnnie had scared Frankie regarding the authorities splitting the two of them up permanently.

"I understand. But she needs temporary help, at least. Social services should be notified soon. They can place her—"

"I'm not a relative. I have no standing. It's not my responsibility to—"

"Then whose is it? It seems like, from what you've told me, that you know and care as much as anybody but her sister. You do have responsibility."

This was Alex all over. She was pretty clear and definite about morality and justice and all that jazz. They were all of a piece. If you could help someone in need or an innocent, you did. It was as simple as that.

I sighed. "I'm going to go and find her tomorrow, and I'll see how she's doing. And I'm hoping for some lucid dreaming tonight, so when I open my eyes in the morning, I'll see the case in a whole new clear light."

"Hmmm. Okay. Good." She pressed back into me and mumbled, "So what do you think might spur your lucidity? Maybe..." She giggled like a schoolgirl and began moving her bottom.

It had been a long time since I'd been offered better inspiration.

CHAPTER 10

I was back in the middle of the pungent jungle again.

I knocked on the psychedelic door and stepped back.

I glanced up at the sky, visible through a gap in the overhanging foliage. Gray and more gray. A persistent drizzle of rain had started at dawn and continued into late morning now. I wore a slick blue parka with a hood and a drenched pair of black jeans.

The door swung open a bit until Maggie caught sight of me. She closed the door, unlatched the chain, and opened it again.

She stood staring at me, her lips slightly parted, her expression slightly vacant. She looked even more disheveled and disoriented than she had yesterday. I wondered what she was on. I'd encountered others like her all too often. Nice girls raised in good families that started running with the wrong crowd or got involved with the wrong man.

Maybe it wasn't as simple as that. It seldom was.

"Maggie, I just came to see Frankie, and she didn't answer downstairs. Is she out again?"

An uncomprehending look greeted my question. Her lips

parted further, her mouth hanging open. For a moment, I wanted to grab her and shake her and tell her to wake up. Time was slipping away, and I was sure she'd already wasted more than her fair share.

But then she blinked her eyes a couple of times, shaking her head, her fingers ticking. A cloud seemed to pass over her face and animation returned. "Oh," she mumbled. "Yes."

I waited.

She closed her mouth, rubbed her lips together, swallowed. "I don't know, Mr...I'm sorry I don't remember—"

"Plank. Max Plank."

"Right. Max. Yes. Nice name. No...I mean I don't know about Frankie. I didn't see her last night or this morning."

"Would you mind if I visited her apartment? I want to leave her a note. It's important that I talk with her."

Maggie nodded, and I stepped by her, hoping that Leonard was out, too.

DOWNSTAIRS I FOUND A DISASTER.

The apartment had been torn apart.

Maggie stood at the edge of the room, her hand over her mouth, her eyes wide open now.

"You didn't hear anything?"

"My god! Who could have done this? Why..."

I looked around. The floor was covered with paper and books, mostly children's—I spotted a hardback copy of *Harry Potter and the Sorcerer's Stone* and cups and other debris. The sofa cushions were slashed open, spilling their white guts. Chairs were turned on their sides, a couple with broken legs. The small television set had been smashed, bits of glass strewn around it on the floor. A bunch of framed paintings were slashed and black and white photos with cracked covers strewn about. One bare wall had lots of empty holes or picture hangers bereft of their hangings. Small statues, replicas of the David and Madonnas and the like, were shattered. Some metal sculptures of what looked like flowers were bent out of shape. I assumed this was part of the art that Johnnie bought online and sold who knows where.

I turned back to Maggie. "Have you been out of the house any time since yesterday?"

"I...no...yes, I just ran down to S&S on the corner for pickles and...some Twinkies." She grinned sheepishly. "I was only gone for...fifteen minutes." Her shoulders slumped, her hands hung like dead tree limbs at her sides.

"Is Leonard here?"

"He's sleeping upstairs in the back bedroom."

"Wake him up."

She bit her lip, looked up at me with hooded eyes.

"Now."

She turned and hurried back up the stairs. I felt dirty somehow as if I was complicit in her submission. She was a woman too used to taking orders from men.

LEONARD STOOD IN THE MIDDLE OF THE ROOM WEARING THE SAME stitched Pendleton, faded jeans, and black boots. He'd ditched the ponytail tie, his hair, grayer when full out, flowed loosely down past his shoulders.

"This is bullshit," he said.

"Honey, I think we'd better wait till—"

"Shhh," he hissed, not looking at her.

Her upper teeth folded over her lower lip, gnawing at the skin beneath. Her eyes bounced like a jackrabbit around the room. "Sweetheart, we have to think about poor Frankie and—"

Leonard turned to her and snarled, "I told you to be quiet, woman."

Her face flushed. She closed her eyes, her lips trembling. I was afraid she was going to cry, but she looked too beaten down even for that.

I could feel the bile at the back of my throat and the anger rising alongside it.

"That little girl..." He stopped, his hands tightening into fists. "I feel for her, but I think she must know something more about all this than she says." His eyes roamed the room, his expression one of utter disdain. "This is going to cost us more than the deposit. The TV alone, Jesus. That sofa cost me two hundred bucks."

"You didn't hear anything?" I said, trying to keep my tone credulous.

"Not a damn thing."

"Maggie says she's been here save for a few minutes when she went to the store. How about you?"

"What is this? You sound like the heat." He looked at me closely, sizing me up. "Who are you really?"

I stared back at him, trying to absorb his use of the word *heat*. I didn't know if he'd watched one too many cop shows on TV, or if he was just lamely trying to project some hipster badass vibe.

"Cut the crap, Leonard."

"What the fuck? This is my house, dammit!"

I'd had enough.

I took a step toward him, and he stumbled backward, startled. It was too late. I grabbed his right arm and wrenched it behind his back, ratcheting it up slowly. "Listen, Lennie, you're starting to piss me off. We're trying to help a little girl here. Somebody broke into your property and busted it up, and Frankie's lucky she wasn't here. Maybe you are, too. If you don't have insurance, then tough luck on the damage. I don't give a shit. Now answer my question."

He twisted from side to side, trying to escape my grasp, but I just kept moving his arm higher until he yelped in pain.

"Mr...Max! Please, don't hurt him. Please!" Maggie cried.

"Shut up, girl," Leonard barked again.

I almost broke his arm then.

"Jeez, fucker! Okay, I was out last night for a few hours."

"Where?"

"What business is that of—Ouch! Alright. Okay. I had a couple of drinks at the Coal Mine and then played cards with my buddies."

"Anything else?

"I was here, man. Other than last night from about eight to midnight, I was here."

"Have you been in the apartment anytime since I was here last?"

"No. Dammit, that hurts!"

"Maggie?"

"Huh?"

"Have you been in here in the last week?"

"No...no...please," she said pitifully.

I let Leonard's arm drop and stepped away.

"Jesus, man, you didn't have to do that."

"Yes, I did," I said, and turned away. I noticed something near the couch, amidst the spilled contents: a small, square, colorful object. I picked it up with a sinking feeling in my chest. Frankie hadn't had time to grab her Rubik's cube. I guessed that she always took it with her, just like her skateboard. The fact that it was still there probably meant she'd had to leave in a hurry.

Or that she hadn't left of her own volition, but been taken away.

I looked back at Leonard, who was rubbing his arm with a pained expression on his face. Maggie stepped closer to him and said, "Are you okay, Len?"

He ignored her and stared at me like I was a crazy, dangerous man.

Perhaps I was.

I left the two of them there to sort out their difficulties. I didn't have much hope that they could, but who am I to pass judgment?

CHAPTER 11

It was 5 p.m. when I walked into a maze of beams and girders, forklifts and front loaders, beneath the Embarcadero Freeway on 3rd Street across from Pier 54.

Marsh had left a message on my cell phone while I was dancing with Leonard and Maggie.

I caught sight of him wearing a white hard hat and a slick blue suit with a cranberry-colored tie, talking to an older man with a set of blueprints rippling in his hands.

Marsh looked up and nodded, and I moved to a corner of the site and sat on the edge of a slab of concrete riddled with rebar. Above me, a half-dozen-men gamboled on high beams like gymnasts, wielding hammers and power drills. The pounding and high-pitched whining filled the cold, crisp sawdust-filled air. Out over the piers, the bay loomed, black and unforgiving. The sun was trying to break through the gloomy cloud cover.

I worried over Frankie, wondering where she was. Whether in hiding or just out on her skateboard somewhere practicing new moves, oblivious to the trouble at home. The Rubik's cube stashed in my motorcycle's saddlebag argued for the former conclusion. I ran back over my conversations with Maggie and Leonard, and the only thing I concluded was that Maggie was with the wrong man, although I knew her nature was part and parcel of the problem. I wondered whether Leonard was used to dominating her, treating her with such dismissiveness, or whether his attitude, his shutting her up, hid more. Was he afraid she was going to say something that might lead me to question his involvement with Frankie and Johnnie and their problems?

"You look nonplussed, Plank."

I looked up. Marsh was standing with his arms folded over his chest, staring out at the ocean.

"What is this?" I waved my hand around the site.

"A yoga center with an Indian vegetarian restaurant that happens to have offices above it."

I don't know what you'd call Marsh. An entrepreneur of a sort. Although most people who worked for him did so on a freelance basis, he employed around twenty people at two offices—-one in North Beach off Columbus Avenue, and the other in Tiburon, with a stunning view of the Bay Area's phantasmagoria. He sometimes developed real estate. Other times he funded small companies that caught his fancy—most recently a new niche coffee shop in Ghirardelli Square called FIX that charged six bucks for a cup. I'd ventured my opinion that this was ridiculous, but most mornings, there was a line of eager caffeine addicts running from FIX's elegant granite counters and elaborate gothic espresso and cappuccino machines out to the brick promenade in front.

Marsh spent a lot his time with martial arts masters and Yogis, deepening his knowledge in those disciplines while working to develop new forms and approaches. He also occasionally did consulting work with secretive government agencies and, I was pretty sure, occasionally participated in clandestine missions that no one ever heard of or likely ever would.

"The yoga here is going to be a combination of Vinyasa and

Iyengar, with a touch of Kripalu and a dash of my own seasoning. I'm going to teach a class now and then."

I nodded. Marsh could twist his body into impossible asanas that hurt to watch.

"Why so serious?" he said, sounding like Heath Ledger from his startling turn as the Joker in *The Dark Knight.*

I smiled. "I've been consorting with the wrong types."

"A hazard in your line of work."

"Too true."

"Anything I should know?"

I filled him in on the break-in at Frankie's apartment and my latest chat with her charming landlords.

"Mr. Chapin?" someone shouted from above.

We both looked up to find two workers, one holding a black-handled hammer and the other balancing a level, staring down at us. Both men were in their twenties, heavily muscled, and projecting a friendly but pronounced macho swagger.

"Yes. Coleman. Castro. What's up?" Marsh called just about everybody by their last name and knew the surnames of everyone who worked for him in any capacity.

"We were just wondering. We made a little wager, boss. Chris was reading an article about you in *The Bay Guardian* that says you made most of your money on Wall Street, investing in stocks and bonds and shit. Speculating." He spouted that word with a barely suppressed edge of disdain. "I say no way, you started real businesses. You had ideas, hired people, did things. That's how you made it. Isn't that right, boss?"

Marsh had an easy camaraderie with his workers that allowed them to take liberties that they wouldn't have dared with your average vastly wealthy tycoon.

"You shouldn't believe everything you read in a rag like that, Coleman," Marsh quipped.

"I told ya, Chris. Boss is no Wall Street guy. He's a straight shooter."

"Shit," Chris muttered.

"Yeah. You're buying me lunch at Cassie's and as much beer as I can drink tonight at Freebo's, buddy." Castro laughed.

Marsh hadn't answered the question, but they were satisfied.

"The Blue Notes happen to have an office not too far from here," Marsh said.

"Tell me more."

We were in a little construction shack on Owens Street. Marsh sat behind a metal desk covered with stained blueprints, used styrofoam cups, scattered multicolored pencils, and a couple of empty Twinkie wrappers.

He explained that he'd found out through his network of contacts in government and political circles that the Blue Notes were far from incognito to the powers-that-be. They were on the police's radar, although so far their activities had not risen to the level of a public crisis that would necessitate a big response. Harassment and on-the-spot pursuit were currently being used to adequate effect, although from what Marsh's contacts gathered, the gang was successful, growing, and flush with money garnered from their primary activities—drugs, with an emphasis on feeding the epidemic in painkiller addiction, and prostitution, along with various protection rackets pressuring small local businesses. It was the latter that most concerned authorities and threatened the greatest retaliation.

He said that top members of the gang were known to hang out at Funky Jack's, a bar on Harrison. It was rumored that two members owned it and that there was an office in back that served as a kind of headquarters for the group.

Caballo Negro, the Black Horse himself, and his minions often gathered there to plan and party.

Marsh didn't know whether Vince and Scooter were among the elite, but it was a place to start.

It was mid-afternoon by then, and Marsh had appointments for the rest of the day.

I only had one, for dinner with Alexandra, but on the basis of that, the memory of our date still potent in my mind, I decided the Blue Notes could wait on us for one more day.

Marsh was going to check the place out tonight, and we tentatively planned to meet here and get over to Funky Jack's at 6 p.m. tomorrow.

I stood to go, but hesitated, standing above him, and said, "How did you make your money? I thought you were a trader when you were merely a callow youth?"

Marsh stared into my eyes for a few seconds, and his expression didn't change from a look of casual nonchalance. "I have been many things, in my youth and out of it. But, my friend, the true story of me and money is full of nuance and complexity. Let's save it for another day."

I nodded and accepted his answer for what it was. I knew that it was all I was going to get until he was ready to give more.

CHAPTER 12

Alexandra's cozy Victorian on Octavia in Pacific Heights was sandwiched between a refurbished mansion and a small apartment building with a neo-gothic exterior currently being converted to tiny condominiums with seven-figure asking prices.

I could smell the garlic, olive oil, and tomato sauce out on her front steps, and it perplexed me.

She opened the door moments after I knocked and kissed me once hard on the lips. She wrapped her arm around my waist and escorted me inside. "I thought we'd eat in tonight."

I liked the idea, but Alexandra almost never cooked beyond French toast for breakfast, her specialty. It wasn't that she couldn't. It was just that the idea of planning a menu was as foreign to her as the intricacies of sewing and origami—both of which she did in her rare spare time—were to me.

"Smells great," I said as we crossed the family room with its blond hardwood floors, pastel-colored couches and chairs, and wainscoted walls.

"You cooked?"

"I wish. It's from this new place, Emilio's, that opened down on Lombard a couple months ago. Their eggplant parm is to die for."

"Hmmm." My mouth was watering, but not for eggplant. Alex wore a loose-fitting top and yoga pants. There wasn't an eggplant parm on Earth that could possibly compete.

I grabbed her, spun her around, and kissed her again for a long time. Finally, she broke my clutch.

"Honey, no. Dinner's almost ready. I've got garlic bread and asparagus and sautéed broccolini and creme puffs from Victoria Pastry for dessert."

"Don't need dessert. I've got you." I reached for her again, but she slipped out of my grasp, laughing, and took my hand, dragging me into the kitchen, but keeping me at arm's length.

EMILIO WAS TO BE CONGRATULATED ON ONE OF THE BEST EGGPLANT parms I'd ever tasted, and I'd sampled more than a few.

We were splitting a custard creme puff, with decaf espresso from Alexandra's Nespresso machine.

Alexandra looked better than all the creme puffs in the world in her black yoga pants and the peach top that I'd been peeking down whenever she leaned over while we ate. She'd catch me and motion naughty naughty with her finger, but with a twinkle in her eye.

"I got a movie," she said, as I sipped the last of my demitasse of espresso.

"Don't want to watch anything but you."

"Tough. I've wanted to see this forever and tonight's the night. It's Paul Thomas Anderson's latest, and I managed to miss it in the theaters."

I sighed.

"You'll get your reward afterward," she said, rising and grabbing our plates. "Help me clean up. The sooner we start the movie, the sooner..." Her voice trailed off suggestively.

THE MOVIE WAS ALMOST WORTH THE WAIT. WHETHER OR NOT IT was a masterpiece, Anderson is the most interesting filmmaker working.

Near the end of the movie, Alexandra's phone hummed and played Pachelbel's Canon, which I knew signaled a call from her editor. She looked at it for a moment but immediately turned back to the screen and let it go to voicemail.

As soon as we'd studied the credits, she picked up her phone and listened. Then she scrunched up her features and gave me a long, sympathetic look.

"No," I said.

"Yes," she responded, with a pout.

"Want to go to the airport with me?"

I said a multisyllabic bad word that made her erupt in laughter.

CHAPTER 13

On the way to the airport, to take my mind off of my disappointment, I filled her in on the case.

"So you don't know where Frankie is now?"

"No," I said, my hands fixed tight on the steering wheel. I was driving her Mazda SUV and would park it back at her house and ride my Ducati home.

"Poor girl. She's all by herself. Her home isn't safe and neither is she. And living with those two...losers, loonies, whatever they are. Max, you have to help her."

All the women in my life seemed to think so. Easier said than done. But I agreed with Meiying and Alexandra. I just had to find her first. I hoped that maybe she'd visit Meiying again. I asked Alexandra to call Meiying to see if Frankie had dropped by.

When we got her on the line, Meiying said no, and Alexandra ended up having to answer queries about what was wrong and why we were asking and if the little girl was in danger. I told Alexandra to tell her that Frankie was safe and had her get off the phone as quickly as she could, which was a bit of a trick with Meiying's relentless interrogation.

My luck to fall in with such caring, determined, daunting women.

Alexandra had carry-on luggage as she was supposed to be gone for only a couple days, looking into a fleeting lead that might dovetail with other clues she'd uncovered in her months-long investigation.

She insisted that I didn't need to accompany her to the gate, that we say goodbye outside the terminal. Our embrace was long, the kiss shorter but no less intense, as we were surrounded by passengers and porters.

As she turned away, she touched my hand and whispered, "I love you."

She looked at me for a moment with passion in her glowing eyes.

I nodded, touched her cheek, kissed her again, mumbling affectionately against her lips.

CHAPTER 14

It was just past midnight when I pulled the Ducati into its space behind the Rusty Root. I took the Rubik's cube out of the saddlebag and shoved it in my jacket pocket.

It was a damp night, full of wayward stars and a pink sliver of a moon. I walked around the back of the shed and angled to the waterfront passing the parade of boats leading to my own.

The ocean on my left hummed in my ear, a briny sea tang filled my nose, people's voices echoed, muted as if they arose from the bottom of a canyon.

I strolled slowly for a half-mile past the U.S.S. Pampanito and Pier 43 1/2, and then the Blue and Gold fleet, and out to Pier 41. Coit Tower, the dying wish of a rich old lady—a paean to the city's firefighters—loomed high on Telegraph Hill, drifting in and out of the fog.

I stepped up onto the *Howl's* deck, spread my arms wide, and yawned even wider. My home was bathed in a dim, kind-of-spooky light from boats nearby and the diffused starlight. I took a step, heard a sound, and stopped abruptly.

I was not the only living creature on my floating home.

The muffled thuds came from below in the cabin. Not a duplicate of my step but closer to the sound of something dropped or knocked over.

I remained motionless and listened.

Soft movements beneath me, audible above the waves slapping the hull.

Perhaps it was the mythical Kraken stirring to life.

I hurried quietly to the edge of the port entry and waited there for a moment, staring into the impenetrable darkness. After a few seconds, I continued around the cabin to the aft side entry, a short stairwell leading to my bedroom.

There was a light switch at the bottom of the stairs, but I couldn't reach it without presenting a looming target to whoever was inside. I had no weapon other than the Rubik's cube. I took it out of my pocket, examined it, hoped it might do some damage in a pinch.

I paused again and listened. All was quiet for a few seconds, and then the silence was broken by a lengthy, plaintive, "Meow."

I let go of my bated breath. It wasn't the first time that a hungry tomcat had made its way onboard. Annoying, but better than a bat or seagull. Either of those could get gnarly.

I descended the stairs, flicked on the light, and found an orange tabby sitting on top of my stove. His black eyes examined me. He didn't seem to like what he saw. He let loose a pissed off meow.

"Cat," I said, "shut up, or I'll turn on a burner and light a fire under your ass."

He meowed again, an even louder complaint.

"Excuse me, pussy, but you're the intruder."

I moved to the fridge, took out a container of almond milk, and poured it into a small bowl. The cat watched every movement, like a cat.

I placed the bowl on the floor. The cat's meow achieved

screech level. He leaped off the stove and plunged into the bowl, his little tongue going a mile-a-minute.

"Mr. Plank."

I spun, gripping the Rubik's cube reflexively, and found her standing behind the couch.

"Frankie," I said, my heart retreating from the middle of my throat.

"I'm sure glad you came back. I didn't know what to do." She glanced down at the tabby, whose face was still deep in the bowl, the lapping tongue rhythmic.

"Thanks for feeding Red. I was just going to do that."

"Your cat?"

"Uh-uh. He just showed up a little while ago."

"His name is Red?"

"Yeah. He looks like a Red, doesn't he?"

I stared at her for a moment. She wore the same jean overalls, but had on a red t-shirt and stained white pants beneath.

Her gaze fixed on my right hand. Her eyes widened. I held the Rubik's cube out to her.

She eagerly took it and immediately began spinning it in her hands.

After a few seconds she stopped, the movement in her hands stilled. She looked up at me. "Where'd you get her?"

"Her?"

"Ruby."

I'd forgotten how animated the world is to kids. Inanimate objects are alive, carrying totemic importance and value. Why wouldn't a Rubik's cube have a name? Especially for a lonely twelve-year-old girl who probably didn't have many or any girl-friends her own age.

"At your apartment."

She held my eyes for a moment, blushed. Looked away. She

looked back down at the cube in her hands and whispered, "I missed you, Ruby."

She sat down on the couch and started working the cube again.

Red finished his milk and commenced rubbing his body around my ankles, slithering between my legs, expressing his temporary affection but mostly just massaging his body after a satisfying meal.

"Are you hungry?" I asked.

She didn't look up at me but nodded her head vigorously up and down.

I PLACED THE SCRAMBLED EGGS, MILK, AND TOAST WITH STRAWBERRY jam down on a folding table in front of the couch. Frankie put Ruby down next to the plate and dove in. She ate like she hadn't had a meal in days. I remembered Alexandra's worry about how the little girl was going to be able to take care of herself.

It only took her a couple of minutes to clean her plate. As she was downing the last of the milk, I said, "How long have you been here?"

She wiped her mouth with the back of her hand. "Since this afternoon. I didn't stay here the whole time, though. I waited for a while to see if you'd come home. But when you didn't, I went to see Meiying. But she wasn't home either. So I just wandered around. There's a skateboard park a ways down there," she jerked her thumb towards the pier, "and I practiced there till it started getting dark. A few hours ago, I came back here."

Red jumped on the couch and into Frankie's lap. She smiled and picked the cat up and hugged it, rubbing her cheek against the rust-colored fur. The cat meowed, pulled free, but allowed himself to be petted as he nestled into Frankie's lap.

"When was the last time you were at your house?"

She scrunched up her face as she scratched behind the cat's ears. "Day before yesterday."

"Where have you been staying?"

She petted Red vigorously, and he moved away, but she grabbed him and held him close against her chest. "Here," she said, giving me an awkward, half-guilty glance.

"Good," I said. I'd been with Alexandra. I was glad I hadn't really locked the boat up tight like I sometimes do. "Tell me about your house."

She had her face in the cat's fur again, but was being gentler and scratching behind his ears at the same time. Red purred.

I knelt beside her, placing a hand on Red's haunches and another on Frankie's shoulder. "I can help you. But you have to tell me everything."

Her chest rose and then fell as she let out a long breath. She mumbled against Red's body, "I'm scared."

I lifted her chin up until her eyes met mine. "Do you know who busted up your house?"

"Uh uh," she said, her eyes forlorn. She wrinkled her brow and added, "You were there?"

"Yes."

"Why?"

"Looking for you."

She nodded, letting the notion settle. At first, it seemed she didn't know what to think about that, but after a few seconds, she smiled. "Okay," she said.

"Okay," I repeated.

"You saw the mess?"

"Uh huh."

"I don't..." She stopped, shook her head, looked down at Red, kept scratching his ears. "Maybe it was Vince or Scooter trying to scare me..."

"You think so?"

She looked up into my eyes, breathed in deeply again, and said, "Naw."

I nodded. "Who do you think then?"

She shrugged, looked up again. "Why would anybody do that to us?"

"Hard to say. I can think of three possible reasons. Either they were trying to steal something, or find something, or trying to scare you. Do any of those make any sense?"

Red jumped off her lap and wandered back to the milk bowl, where more lapping ensued.

Frankie grabbed the Rubik's cube and more twisting ensued.

"Was anything missing?"

"Don't think so."

"So it probably wasn't a robber. That leaves someone trying to find something that you might have or someone just trying to scare you. Can you think of anybody who might be involved in either of those?"

The Rubik's cube slowed, paused, stopped.

I tapped her on the knee, crawling forward until I was looking up into her face. "I'll protect you no matter what. But you need to tell me what you know or just what you think might be happening."

"I don't get it though." She was looking straight at me now, her eyes narrowed like she was trying to decipher a particularly vexing problem. "Why'd he have to destroy our apartment? He could have just asked me..."

"Who could have asked you?"

"You promise not to tell him I told you?"

I nodded my chin.

"Leonard," she said, biting off the name with a sulfurous snarl.

"Leonard was trying to scare you?" A surge of gloom rose in my chest.

"Not scare me. But maybe looking for something."

Even though Leonard seemed to me a weasel, it didn't make sense that he'd bother busting up the place, breaking his own stuff, if he was trying to find something Frankie had. "What do you think he was looking for?"

"A list."

"Of what?"

"Names of people."

I immediately thought I could guess what she might be talking about, but before I could say anything, Frankie added, "Maybe it's not him. It's crazy. 'Course he's crazy sometimes. So's Maggie. But I feel sorry for her cuz he can be so mean."

"So what was this list and how did you get it?"

"I did it for Johnnie—but she didn't know!" She looked up at me with those big eyes that urged me to believe that what she was saying was the truth. "First I thought it might be on his computer, but it wasn't cuz he was too scared to put it there. I searched that while he was gone one time. I found some yucky porn, but no list."

A memory flashed in my mind: finding nudie magazines in my father's closet at home when I was ten or eleven years old. It was a shocker, and I looked at Dad differently for a while after that. It shamed me, but also gave me a weird sense of power or, more accurately, control. Dad was a no-nonsense guy with a hair-trigger temper who brooked no impertinence from his only son. I felt like, for once, I had a little something on him, some leverage that I might use some day. It was silly and ridiculous, of course, the naive fantasies of a pre-adolescent boy.

Suddenly a revelation extinguished the memory in a flash. I almost slapped my forehead. Leonard's computer triggered it. Why hadn't I thought of it before? Frankie had mentioned Johnnie's online business, and Leonard had confirmed it.

"Frankie, Johnnie had a computer, didn't she?"

"Course. Laptop. Aces."

"Do you know where it is?"

"At home. Johnny usually puts it in a drawer in her desk and locks it. She takes good care of it and is always afraid somebody might break in and steal it." Frankie nodded her head up and down. "Guess she was right to be worried."

"So you think the person who broke in took it?"

"I don't know. I didn't notice. She's got the key to the drawer hidden, so maybe not."

"Do you know where the key is?"

"Sure. It's on top of the tall bookcase, tucked into a corner."

I nodded. If I could get my hands on Johnnie's laptop, the information there might help clear up murky matters and illuminate shady characters. Another trip to Leonard and Maggie's was in the offing, and the thought depressed me. But I shook that off and asked Frankie to continue her story.

"So I didn't give up. I watched Leonard when he wasn't paying attention, looking for clues. One night I went upstairs, and he was on the phone in the kitchen, talking real angry and shaking a piece of paper in his hand. I stayed in the hall and waited till he hung up. He swore, looked at the paper, then reached up above the 'fridgerator and put it inside the middle of a big cookbook that was full of dust cuz nobody ever uses it. I tiptoed downstairs before he could see me and waited for a while till I was sure he'd gone to bed."

She stopped and looked at me.

"You went back and took it?"

"Uh huh," she said with a conspiratorial gleam in her eye.

"Weren't you afraid he'd get upset when he saw it was missing?"

"Sure. I just wanted to show it to Johnnie, but she stayed out all night that night and didn't come back in the morning. So I went down to the copy shop a couple of blocks away and made two copies. I went straight back home and was going to put it back in the book, but all heckola had already broken out."

"He found it missing?"

"Yeah. And he was screaming and yelling at Maggie, who was acting like a mouse as usual. God, if I ever have a husband who talks to me like that, I'm going to brain him with my skateboard. I felt so sorry for her I almost ran upstairs and spilled the beans, but I was afraid he'd kick us out and then we'd have nowhere to go." She paused, confusion and helplessness written all over her face. "After a while, he came downstairs and screamed at me too, but I just sat there and acted dumb. He looked like he was going to explode, and he was cursing everybody, including himself, for being so 'effing stupid."

"When was this?"

She crooked her mouth, rolled up her eyes, and said, "Maybe two weeks ago."

"How long after that did Johnnie disappear?"

This question startled her. Her eyes widened, her skin blanched, and she swallowed. "I don't...a few days before..." She shook her head, trying to absorb this new notion that she hadn't previously considered as being part of the puzzle's mix.

"Hadn't you thought that the list and Johnnie's disappearance might be connected?"

"No, cuz Johnnie was so upset about Scooter and Vince screwing her and she went after them so...I don't think that's true. I don't think the list or Leonard did anything to Johnnie."

"You said Johnnie didn't know you took the list?"

She shook her head.

"But you must have known it was something she wanted."

"I'd heard them talking about it. Johnnie asked him if she could see it because it would really help her with her business. But he said no way. They argued for a while, and he said a bunch of nasty things to her. Course, being Johnnie, she was nasty right back. She doesn't put up with shit from anybody, especially men." Frankie smiled, proud of her big sister.

Outside somebody in a nearby boat turned on music. At least they had taste. It was Sinatra, singing in his dusky late night voice. *In the Wee Small Hours of the Morning.*

"So after that's when you decided to find the list to help her?"

"Sure. It took me a while, but I did it."

"What was on the list?"

She shrugged. "Names, email addresses, phone numbers. Other numbers—some about money. One thousand. Five Thousand. Ten Thousand. I didn't understand it, really. There was also these strange descriptions about women next to some of the names. Blonde. Brunette. Legs. Tits. Stuff like that. It was really weird and creeped me out, especially after I saw some of the stuff on Leonard's computer." Frankie blushed and wrinkled her nose.

She wasn't the only one creeped out. "Were most of the names on the list men?"

"Yeah. But there were at least five or six women."

"How many total?"

"Mmmm...maybe twenty or so."

"What did Frankie say when you showed her the list?"

"I didn't. Not at first. When she got home later in the morning, she was really tired, and Leonard came roaring downstairs accusing her of taking the list, but he knew she didn't, just by the way she was acting. He yelled at her anyway, and she yelled back, and he left after a while. He went out. Johnnie went to bed, and Maggie was hiding out in her room. I tiptoed upstairs and put the list back in the book."

This little girl had chutzpah to spare. I was a little in awe, and if her big sister was anything like her, she would be formidable, particularly with her looks to boot. But their guts, their ballsy savvy, had also gotten them into terrible trouble, and things might get worse yet.

"Was Leonard happy when he found it?"

"He didn't say much. I was hoping he'd figure that he'd just missed it the first time, but I think he was still suspicious. He was careful about some things, and he didn't trust anybody. I bet he still thought Johnnie took it and maybe that's why he messed up our apartment, looking for a copy and going crazy when he didn't find it, and breaking things without thinking how nuts it was. He has this crazy temper...like..." She glanced up at me for a moment before saying, "...a lot of men do."

I nodded. I couldn't disagree with her. She and Johnnie probably already had to bear the brunt of too much male frustration and anger.

"When you showed her your copy of the list, what did Johnnie say?"

"It wasn't until that night, after dinner. She couldn't believe it. She got mad at me. But I could tell it made her happy. She was just worried about me, what Leonard might do if he caught me. But I didn't care. I only cared what Johnnie thought."

"Did she ever tell you anything about the list?"

"She said it was about business. She said that Leonard promised to give her the names, but he went back on his promise. Just like Scooter and Vince." She paused, frowned, looking up at me with longing eyes. "Mr. Plank, why are so many adults liars?"

There was no easy answer to the little girl's question. Lying is so prevalent, so permeates everyday life that people, I think, just take it as a given or don't notice it at all. Lies are the prime currency of business executives and politicians. A reassuring mythology that envelops us in a seldom-pierced insulation of good feeling, the very ocean that we swim in. Television lies to us thousands of times a day in order to sell us stuff we don't need and don't know we don't want.

It wasn't just two-bit hustlers like Leonard, and maybe Frankie's own sister, who used lies as currency. American progress, for good and bad, has always been built on lies and sustained by a general ignorance of our own history.

Frankie looked tired, and she wasn't the only one, so I made up a cot and left her and the cat sleeping. I went up on deck and had a tall shot of whiskey and listened to Sinatra croon across the water about lost love and loose women and lonely nights.

CHAPTER 15

In the morning, I found a can of pumpkin in the cupboard and used that and some nutmeg and buttermilk to whip up pancakes, along with bacon. Coffee for me, cranberry juice for Frankie. More almond milk for the cat.

"Shouldn't we get Red some real cat food?" Frankie asked as she poured another healthy dollop of syrup over her already soaked stack.

"If he hangs around. Maybe he belongs to somebody else around here. One of the other boat owners." I doubted that, but I could hope.

"He doesn't. I don't think he has a home at all." She reached down and petted the cat, who ignored her and continued slurping the milk.

"Well, we'll see. I'll pick up a small bag of cat food later."

That seemed to satisfy her, and she dug back into her pancakes.

AFTER BREAKFAST, FRANKIE INSISTED ON DOING THE DISHES, AND

she did a thorough job and handed me the clean-as-a-whistle plates to dry.

As we were finishing up, Meiying popped her head into the galley.

"Max, you have new dishwasher?"

Frankie screeched and ran into Meiying's arms. They hugged, pulled back, stared at each other with big smiles, hugged again.

She and Dao had never had kids. Dao had informed me, in his usual blunt manner, that his sperm count was too low. They'd thought about adoption, but life had somehow gotten in the way as for many years they'd led a peripatetic existence: Dao working for or consulting with various mighty giants of finance from New York to London to Hong Kong to Dubai, until finally he'd gotten tired of the bullshit and hooey of high finance and gone off on his own, settling finally onto the *Sweet and Sour*, falling in love with San Francisco and its peerless bay.

All that to say, a baby never happened. They might have some regrets about that, but it didn't seem to impact their powerful bond.

As I watched Frankie and Meiying, my cell phone rang from across the room. I took it out of my jacket and went out onto the deck above, leaving the girls to their pleasant chatter.

The sky was a vast and mostly blue canvas. It was cool with a slight southwesterly breeze. A brown pelican sat regally on the post of a pier, with a flock of seagulls circling overhead anxious for a mid-morning snack.

"Plank," I said into the phone.

"Yeah. This is Leonard, you know."

It wasn't a question. Neither he nor I was likely to forget each other for a while, an unfortunate reality for both of us. For a moment, I wondered how he'd gotten my number, but then I remembered giving him my card.

"I do know," I answered.

"I want the girl out of here," he said. Well, howdy-do to you too, Len.

"What are you talking about?"

"You know what I mean. C'mon man, it's too dangerous around here. Johnnie was into some serious shit, and now Frankie's up in it. Why should I be involved? It's already cost me more than five hundred bucks and—"

"Why are you calling me?"

There was a pause on the line. I could hear his wheezy breath as he considered my question.

"I haven't seen her, man, but I don't want her coming back here. I figured you'd know where she was and you could talk to her, tell her what's up."

"You're a prince among men, Lenny. Do you have a lease signed by Johnnie?"

Another pause while he decided whether to lie or not. "There was a lease, but it expired. I can throw 'em out anytime I want."

That was bluster and he knew it. "That's not the way it works. You have to give thirty days' written notice."

"Bullshit, man. Bullshit," he repeated as if trying to hammer home the fact that he knew he was full of it. "I want her out. If she comes back, she's going to have it rough here. I'm telling you, I'm going to—"

"Shut up. If she comes back, you aren't going to do a damn thing to that little girl. If I find out that you so much as raised your voice to her, I'm going to pay you a visit, and we're going to resume our previous chat." Leonard was a hustler, and a low-life, and a true creepazoid. And like all vermin of his nature, he was a coward.

"I'm not afraid of you, man. If you start up with that shit you tried last time, strong-arming me, I'm gonna call the cops."

I laughed. I couldn't help it. "I didn't mention any kind of violence. I just said we'd chat. And I'd welcome the police. If they aren't already aware of some of the activities going on at your lovely home, I'm sure they'll be interested in your business."

"God damn you. I've got friends. Tough as you for sure." His voice trailed off. "Shit," he muttered under his breath, emitting a low growl of frustration. "I don't want the kid back here. Tell her that."

"Goodbye, Lennie," I said, and heard him mumble, "Dammit," as I tapped the phone off.

The pelican had joined the seagulls in the sky and suddenly veered sharply downward and dove, in that inimitable rocket-like way, until it plunged into the water, breaking the surface with a splash of white foam. A moment later, it emerged with a mouthful of anchovies.

I'd thought about mentioning the list that Frankie had stolen from him. I could do it without implicating her, and it would probably really throw him into a panic. I assumed it was a list containing the names of his drug clientele, along with some of their "preferences" in women, which put an interesting spin on his business, and my view of his relationship with Maggie. I still didn't know enough to make a firm conclusion, but things were beginning to go from opaque to merely murky. I'd decided to hold off on confronting him with my knowledge of the list until an appropriate moment when we were face-to-face, and I'd have a much better shot at breaking through his inevitable prevarications.

My thoughts were interrupted by Meiying calling me from below. "Plank, I want to take Frankie to the *Sweet and Sour* with me. Big plans today."

"Big plans!" Frankie giggled, and Meiying shushed her, but they both laughed even louder, delighted with their secrets.

Plans which solved my problem of what to do with Frankie for the moment. I was sure that Meiying and Dao would take the girl in, at least for a couple of days.

I was also sure Leonard couldn't evict her as quickly as he hoped, but I was as worried as he pretended to be about the danger she was in. Until I could figure out what was going on, I'd keep her close to me.

If anything happened to Frankie, I knew I'd have to answer to Meiying and Alexandra, and that was almost as frightening as the prospect of the unseen forces gathering around the little girl.

CHAPTER 16

"So what did Tom say to that?"

Marsh frowned. He picked up his white bone china demitasse cup of rich, in all senses of the word, seven buck espresso. He took a sip and smiled.

I had my bargain basement, six-dollar Americano in front of me, held within the confines of a black mug with the store logo—a dancing woman with a wrench in one hand and a cup of coffee in the other—etched in gold across its surface.

It was early evening. We'd had dinner at the Rusty Root, and we were at FIX in Ghirardelli Square—one of three locations, with three more planned to open in the next few months, according to Marsh, who was an investor and part owner/consultant to the three twenty-something fledgling entrepreneurs, who were intent on pushing the envelope vis-a-vis how much you could charge for a cup of coffee and still keep a straight face.

Judging by the size of the crowd wending its way out the door, the sky's the limit.

I sometimes marveled at the continuing influx of people from all over the world anxious to call the Bay Area home. The real estate prices were beyond ridiculous, the traffic horrendous, and places like FIX stretched the bounds of the fantastic.

Beauty has its price, and the gorgeous lady that is San Francisco is a demanding bitch.

"So?" I said after it looked like Marsh wasn't going to answer my question.

"I like him. I do. But he's gotten too possessive. He's young. He doesn't realize there's a big old world out there and that I'm not his knight in shining armor."

"Want me to clue him in for you?"

"Thanks. But I've already done that. He's familiar with the negative side of my ledger and doesn't seem to care."

"You're such a lovable lug, it's hard to see your forest for your trees."

Marsh studied a couple of young surfer types at the counter eating gluten-free kale and cranberry muffins and drinking organic green tea, perhaps steeped in Himalayan spring water, hand-carried by extra virgin Sherpas down from the snowy peaks.

"So what's the verdict?"

"Huh?" He eyed the younger surfer, probably only around twenty, with golden locks and a deep tan, wearing a purple headband, three gold earrings in his right ear, and a shirt open to the waist revealing chiseled pecs, hot out of a Tony Horton commercial.

"Yes," he said, finally, reluctantly looking away from the hunk. "He's moving out, but we're still going to talk. He insists we try a..." Marsh made parentheses with his fingers, "'timeout' but that we talk every other day and meet for dinner once a week while we figure things out."

"Sounds very adult. And you went along with it?"

"Even though it's a waste of time. I don't know how long I can bear with it, but I'll try. In the meantime, let's—"

The surfers rose, and as they moved by our table, Marsh called out to them. "Gentlemen, may I have a word with you."

They stopped, looked around, then decided that he was speaking to them. He coaxed them closer with a wagging index finger.

"Thanks, gents. I'm Marsh Chapin, and this is my friend, Plank. I was just wondering, if you don't mind, what you thought of the muffins and the tea. I work with the owners here, and those are new items on the menu. There's nothing like immediate feedback, no?" he said, smooth as smooth ever gets.

"Yeah, sure," the older, shorter one replied with a smug expression on his face. He was happy to be consulted. He had thinning black hair, a goatee, a dark tan, and wore a Hawaiian shirt. He was in good shape, but paled in every way next to his younger buddy.

As he sang the praises of gluten free and organic, Marsh and the blond Adonis eyed each other frankly.

After goateed finished, Marsh said, "Thank you, Mr.?"

"It's George. And this is Dave."

"Dave, nice to meet you," Marsh said. "And what did you think of the fare, David?"

"It was okay," he said, coolly. It was obvious Dave understood the value and heft of what stared back at him in the mirror every morning. He wasn't going to be reeled in so easily by an attractive stranger's offhand pitch.

"Good," Marsh said. "Thank you for your time." He opened his wallet, extracted a couple of cards. "Here's my contact information. If you have any suggestions regarding the shop, please don't hesitate. We really want to involve the community in making this the best coffee establishment in town."

Marsh stood, shook George's hand, then turned to the beautiful Dave and gripped his hand, at the same time placing his other palm around the younger man's wrist. "A pleasure," Marsh said, staring into his eyes. "I do hope to hear from you."

You could see a light bulb clicking on, a dawning on George's face as to what had just happened. Marsh stepped back, sat down, and asked me if I wanted another coffee. I nodded, and he motioned to the barista.

Surfer boys stood by the table for a few seconds in silent reverie, considering perhaps the ramifications of the encounter and what might occur as a result. Marsh ignored them as if they no longer existed.

Finally, Dave said, "Let's go."

I was sure that, before twenty-fours passed, Dave would think of something that might improve FIX in some small, yet interesting way, and feel an immediate need to call Marsh.

FUNKY JACK'S LIVED UP TO ITS NAME.

It reeked of cigarette smoke, cheap whiskey, a strong dose of unwashed man, and a skosh of urine.

It was a narrow low-ceilinged space holding three rooms: The first was a small foyer, complete with an ancient crystal chandelier that hung so low that anyone taller than five-and-a-half feet had to veer around it or suffer a bloody nose. A massive antique coat rack with copper-colored hangers took up most of the space. The walls were covered with dark paintings of the English countryside, Romantic-era landscapes and ocean scenes in the J.W. Turner style. The floor was black marble.

This makes the room sound fancy, but it wasn't. Most of the chandelier lights were broken and filthy, the coat rack was covered with jackets, blouses, men's and women's underwear—a black bra and tangerine colored thong the most prominent—and old shoes. A thick veneer of dust covered the paintings. The floor was cracked, cratered, perilous to step on.

The main room appeared to have no relation to the entry. It was a long, dark space, with a vinyl covered bar on the left that spanned the length of it. A dozen tables were scattered about in no discernible pattern. The floor was hard-bitten wood and sawdust, the ceiling painted black. A large, smoky black mirror centered the bar. The decorations featuring motifs from the Mexican Day of the Dead: skulls, unlit and half-melted candles, dolls with cadaverous faces, and cheap costume jewelry scattered about.

The bar was fronted by a half-dozen swiveling stools with either ripped or faded black leather covers. The only light in the room was provided by a few bulbs in cast iron fittings.

The air was full of smoke and broken dreams.

Overall, the place was a nice mashup of a coal mine and a whorehouse.

When Marsh and I entered, all heads, ten including the bartender, turned toward us and gawked.

We ignored the startled looks and wandered to the bar. I ordered a beer and Marsh a coffee, black. The bartender—young, bald, Asian, hostile—gave Marsh a look of disdain and said, "Coffee, man?"

Marsh gave him a look back, and the bartender shrugged. "Got some from this morning. I can heat it back up for you if you want."

"As appealing as that sounds, I'd like a fresh cup, please," Marsh purred.

"Jesus." He looked toward the ceiling, unable to comprehend the trials that God was sending his way. "Okay," he mumbled. "Be ten minutes. At least."

"Great to see that fine service is still valued in this great city," Marsh said to no one in particular, turning his back to the bar.

At a corner table, three older men, two drinks past woozy, sat hunched and muttering over a game of liar's dice. At another table near the entry sat three young women, all Latino, all with short skirts, spiky heels, and black stockings. The table was covered with empty shot glasses and full ashtrays, and the women leaned in close to each other, trading secrets, stealing glances.

The sharp unmistakable crack of a break shot came from behind us, and after I got my pint, we wandered back to take a closer look.

The two pool tables were worn but in decent shape, seemingly the only objects that received a modicum of care in the establishment.

Six young men with pool cues surrounded the tables. The men were all young—all sharp elbows and puffed-out chests, tough talk, and dirty jokes.

It took me a few moments to notice the two men lurking at the farthest corner of the room, shadowy figures in the dim light. One sat on a tall bar stool backed up against a closed door. The other knelt beside him, occasionally making comments to which the seated man nodded. I couldn't make out their features, but I felt a dangerous vibe emanating from them.

The boys were shooting separate games of eight ball for money. Piles of twenty dollar bills sat at the tables' edges. There was a squirrelly bite to the conversation, the typical blasphemous cursing and macho posturing, back slapping, goading. It was friendly but tinged with the barely concealed hint of violence.

Marsh and I watched silently. After a long while, the bartender called out that the coffee was ready, and Marsh brought back a mug full and winced when he took a sip.

"Not up to FIX standards, eh?"

"If he didn't just reheat the stuff he made this morning, you can't tell. Course it probably was dreck in the first place."

The pool players paid no particular attention to us, although there was the occasional glance or brief appraisal beneath hooded eyes.

After ten minutes, a fat young Mexican kid with a full beard pointed his pool cue, moving it back and forth between us. "Hey man," he said.

I looked at him but said nothing.

"You play or just watch."

"I haven't played for a while, but I used to."

"You like to gamble?" another man said. This one was tall and lanky, loaded with tattoos.

I shrugged.

Lanky said, "Scooter, you wanna play 'em?"

Scooter stepped in front of the table and planted his cue stick. He dropped the cigarette dangling from his right hand to the floor and ground it out with a dismissive twist of the toe of his black silver-buckled boot. A gunslinger posturing before a duel.

He wore black jeans and a black t-shirt and looked like his little brother, Louie, only with a more pronounced epicanthic fold to his Asian eyes, fewer tattoos, and more hair. The long black tresses trailed to his shoulders.

"Your friend play?"

"I prefer shuffleboard," Marsh quipped.

Scooter gave him a quizzical look. Marsh raised his hands, palms up, in a "sorry but I'm just a square peg who happens to live in a round-hole-world" gesture.

"Choose your weapon, man," the fat Mexican said, pointing to the wall opposite the pool tables—a rack with a dozen or so cues.

After sampling a few, I decided on one made out of maple that seemed to have the hardest tip and lightest weight of the bunch. I checked out the balance point with two fingertips. It was a few inches ahead of the wrap.

"What you doin' man," the Mexican mocked. "Picking out a dress?"

Everybody got a laugh out of that one. Me too.

THE FIRST GAME WAS SHORT AND TO THE POINT.

Scooter extended me the courtesy of the first break and then sunk a solid ball, followed by two more before he missed.

I then sunk all my striped balls, called the black ball to a corner pocket, and sunk that one, too.

The second game followed the same pattern, only more directly.

It didn't take long for the boys to start grumbling.

I'd won almost a thousand bucks, and my new friends thought that perhaps they'd been hustled. They were young and fancied themselves wise in the ways of the world.

"You're pretty good man," the Mexican, Marco, said.

Scooter had been silent throughout and was now standing with his cue held out in front of him, another cigarette dangling from his lips, his dark brown eyes studying me with possible malice aforethought.

"Just lucky, I guess. Haven't played for a while," I said.

"Bullshit," Scooter mumbled.

I nodded. "That's one way to look at it. You asked me to play."

"You stood there waiting for us to ask, man. You set us up," the lanky boy, Jeff, spat.

The troops were restless and moving forward around the table. Only one of them hung back. I'd heard somebody call him Vince—another Latino, probably from Central America, who looked nervous and out-of-place. He glanced in the corner toward the two men in the shadows, then looked back to me with a fearful expression on his face.

I remembered the grocer, Jalil, telling me about Vince, that he was the only good one of the bunch.

I glanced down at the table and noticed the pile of money sitting on the rail, supposedly a little more than a thousand dollars, but I didn't bother to count it. I grabbed it, stuffed it in my pocket, and stepped away.

STRAY CAT BLUES   115

"Looks like nobody else wants to try their luck," I said. They looked surprised that I'd dare pocket my winnings.

"Put the money back, asshole," Scooter snapped.

"You'll have to pry it from my cold, dead hands," I tried with a smile on my face.

"Oh, Plank, please," Marsh groaned.

"He's fuckin' with you, man. Are you gonna take that disrespect?" The rabble-rouser was a mammoth slab of youthful arrogance. Full of piss and vinegar blended with gaping stupidity. Its name was Frank, and Frank's eyes were crazy for a fight.

Scooter squared his shoulders and grabbed his pool cue with both hands. A medieval warrior girding his sword.

I took another step back and found myself side-by-side with Marsh.

"I must warn you, gentlemen. My friend here is rather adept in nasty practices that, despite your obvious experience and formidable heft, you may have never before encountered. And, not to boast, but I myself am learned in the pugilistic arts."

"Plank," Marsh repeated, his disappointment intensifying with my every word.

"Who the hell are you?" Marco said, shaking his head like he couldn't believe we were actually standing there, daring disaster. In that den of wolves.

Scooter rushed me, his pool cue aiming for my solar plexus. I side-stepped him, pivoted, hooked his left ankle with the toe of my right foot. He fell flat on his face.

Frank was next and, for his size, surprisingly quick. He was almost upon me when he crumbled to the ground with an agonized cry. He bounced on the floor like a giant Mexican jumping bean, clutching his stomach, growling, inventing a new language, a primitive tongue appropriate to his atavistic state. Marsh stood calmly behind him. I hadn't seen what he'd thrown at the poor boy.

Scooter jumped to his feet, holding his bloody nose. He grabbed my arm, threw a punch. I deflected it with my elbow and hit him hard in the gut. He collapsed again.

As I turned, I noticed Marco moving toward us. He had a thin-handled blade in his hand, waving it back and forth. "You mother—"

Marsh stopped the expletive in his throat. I can't say that I saw what really happened. Marsh was in the air, the knife flew across the room, and Marco hit the ground hard. Then Marsh was back beside me, sighing. It happened in the blink of an eye.

Marco was out cold. He'd been lucky. He'd be hurting when he woke up, but not as much as Frank, who would likely never forget the day he met Marsh.

Two other men clutched their cue sticks but stayed in place. Vince stood impassively, staring down at the floor.

"Good game," I said.

"What do you want?" The voice was strong, commanding. It belonged to the seated man in the corner.

"Just want to take my winnings and move on. Thought we were just having a friendly game of eight-ball."

In response, the man who had been kneeling next to the speaker's voice came out of the shadows. He was holding a snub-nosed revolver and keeping a considerable distance between himself and Marsh. Smart boy.

"Put the money back on the table and get the hell out of here, or Ernie will pry it out of your cold, dead pockets."

"Touché," I said. "Still, I'm surprised. This looks like such a nice establishment, and you look like such fair-minded young men. I won fair and square."

"We don't like outside hustlers coming in here and cheating us." There was a long pause while he let that settle in. "You're lucky, Mr. Plank. You deserve worse than just giving up money that isn't yours. And I'd advise that you and your friend scratch

Funky's off your address lists. Pretend like it doesn't exist. 'Cuz for you, it doesn't." Another misspent youth learning how to speak from watching Vin Diesel movies.

But I wondered why he wasn't pressing his advantage right then. It wasn't as great as it looked, not with Marsh in the room, but I was pretty sure they didn't want any violence that might draw the attention of the authorities to their little home away from home. I'd actually counted on that but knew that it wouldn't provide any absolute guarantee of safety. Ergo, Marsh was with me.

"Okey-dokey," I said and reached in my pocket. I noticed Ernie's finger tighten a little on the trigger. I smiled at him, took out the money, and threw it on the pool table. "Not very sporting, if you ask me."

I turned to Marsh and said, "Watson, my friend, it appears our time here is at an end."

"No shit, Sherlock," Marsh quipped, and we ambled out of that den of miscreants.

CHAPTER 17

W e'd rattled the hive, and it didn't take long for the bees to fly away.

I attributed it to mortification. What Marsh and I had done in there had to be a blow to the collective gang ego. We were two; they were four times that number. We were old; they were young. We were strangers; this was their home field. They had all the advantages, yet they'd gotten their butts kicked, literally, and in their chosen tests of masculinity—eight ball and hand-to-hand combat. They were probably having a hard time playing the macho dudes they fancied themselves to be. Best to go home and have your momma or your woman heal the wounds and reassure that you were still a big, tough boy.

We took turns on lookout. One of us would stay at the car parked a long block away while the other hung out in a dark alley right across the way from Funky Jack's.

Scooter left with Frank in an old Oldsmobile raked and decked out with colossal fins.

Vince was one of the last to leave. Only Ernie, and the assumed leader, Caballo Negro, and the bartender remained inside.

He took a sharp left outside the bar and walked quickly down 9th street. He stopped in front of an old blue VW bug and inserted a key in the driver's side door.

Before he could lean in, I reached him.

"Vince," I whispered in his ear. "Like to talk to you."

He flinched, pulled back, his right hand starting toward his pocket. I grabbed his wrist, twisting his palm back to an angle it was never meant to reach. "Not a good idea."

He cried out and shot me a panicked look. Words scampered out of his mouth. "I didn't have nothing to do with what went on in there. You won. I know. Talk to Scooter or Marco or..." His voice trailed off, his mind catching up with the danger of saying too much more. I released his hand.

"I don't care about the game or the money. I just have a few questions."

"I don't know anything." He glanced nervously back toward the club while rubbing his wrist. "Shit, man. That hurt."

I nodded, acknowledging his pain. "You and Scooter know Johnnie."

He frowned, looked away, held up his hands, palms up. "No. I don't know nuthin'."

"I can go get my friend Marsh. He's a little pissed off about being cheated out of a thousand bucks we won fair and square. He's kind of aching to take it out on somebody."

"Shit," he mumbled.

I walked around to the passenger side of the VW and opened the door. "Get in. Let's take a little drive, or do you want to stand here and talk? Maybe Caballo Negro will come out, and we can all chat together."

"Dammit." He glanced back again. With a pained look on his face, he said, "Okay. Five minutes. Then I gotta go." He sat behind the wheel, and I slid in beside him. He started the car and drove around the corner. I had him continue on and make a loop around the block. We ended up parking behind Marsh's car, a hundred yards from Funky Jack's.

After he shut off the engine, I turned to face him.

He stared straight ahead through the windshield, clutching the steering wheel.

"I've heard some good things about you, Vince, but you've got bad taste in friends."

"What the hell?" he muttered.

"Met your brother. Is he running the car repair business now?"

Vince's head jerked to face me. He grimaced. "Louie?"

"Yep. He seems an industrious lad."

"Why..."

"Looking for you."

"Leave him out of this. He's got nothing to do with any of this." He closed his eyes and shook his head. "He's a good kid. I promised our grandma that I'd take care of him...shit."

So he did have an ounce of decency left in him, a caring for his own flesh and blood, if not his fellow man.

But I wasn't going to allay his fears in any way, at least not until he leveled with me. "Tell me about your business with Johnnie."

"I can't talk about that. You know, I mean Scooter would...I just can't...."

"You bought stuff from her, right? Paintings. Statues. Are you one of those closet art lovers? I wouldn't have guessed, but people can surprise you. Maybe your friends wouldn't understand your love of fine art so you kept it a secret."

He shook his head, closed his eyes. "Caballo doesn't know."

"He doesn't care for art?"

"The bitch set us up."

"Explain."

Outside the streets were deserted, the night still, save for a homeless guy, tottering on his feet, his hands sunk in a garbage can at the lip of the alley, kitty corner to us.

I could see Marsh's head reclining back on the rest, his eyes on the rearview mirror, more than likely listening to some long dead Italian or German composer.

Vince turned to look at me. "Who you working for?"

"A friend."

"What you wanna know?"

"Like I said, I want to know about the business between Johnnie and you and Scooter."

"What for?"

"Why you think?"

"How the damn hell should I know?" He looked back out the front window, keeping his eyes on the front of Funky Jack's, his thoughts on how he could get away with telling me as little as possible.

"Cut the bullshit. You know Johnnie disappeared. I know she was pissed as hell at you for trying to rip her off. She came to see you to get the money she was owed, and then she vanished. What did you do to her?"

He slapped the dashboard hard. "She screwed us, man."

"So you killed her," I said.

"No! No way." He scratched the back of his neck, frowned, his facial muscles twitching.

"I'm getting bored. Maybe I'll just whisper something to one of my friends, a detective with the police department, about your involvement with the missing girl and let them pick you up. Or— and this is what I'd advise if, God forbid, I was you—tell me your side of the story, and we can avoid all that muss and bother and jail time."

He opened his mouth, stopped, clamped his lips shut. I waited for a long time, letting the pressure build.

He glanced over at me, then looked away when I caught his eye.

"Are you working for..." He worried his lower lip with his teeth, then managed to get the word out. "Poe?" An agonized look on his face accompanied the word. I was reminded of the fear induced by the name Voldemort in the Harry Potter books.

I thought about the question. If I were working for Poe and Vince refused my request, it didn't bode well for his future health, and he and I both knew it.

"Poe cares about this. Do you want to have a chat with him?"

"That's what we were afraid of. That's why I came with you. That bitch somehow got close to the man."

I, too, was afraid of Poe's involvement with this whole affair. If he was more tied to it than he'd let on, everything was going to be a lot more complicated to unravel and deal with. Not to mention more dangerous to the health and well-being of all concerned, including one Max Plank.

I let out a long intentionally exasperated and hopefully fore-boding breath. "Last chance. My patience is gone. If you don't want to get a lot more involved with the police and Poe, I suggest you tell me what was going on between you and Johnnie and what happened the last time she came to see you."

He mimicked my sigh, but, I felt, with much less dramatic bravado. "Okay. But I don't know what you're talking about with that art stuff."

"She sold you paintings, sculptures, art, right?"

"No." He looked at me with a sincere you-must-be-crazy expression on his face.

"So you weren't working some art scam with her?"

He shook his head and laughed with a grimace. "Course not. What would we do with that stuff?"

I remembered the wall of art in Frankie's apartment. The paintings slashed and scattered on the floor, the empty wall with

STRAY CAT BLUES 123

holes and picture hangers, the sculptures and metal figurines broken and twisted. I'd assumed it was stuff Johnnie hadn't gotten around to selling off.

"So Johnnie never brought you any artwork to sell for her?"

"Naw."

"Did you know her apartment was full of it?"

"How would I know, man? I never visited her." He paused, reflecting. "But I guess I knew she liked it. She mentioned it every once in a while. How she'd bought a painting or statue or something that she really liked. But she never tried to pawn any stuff off on us. If she had, we'd have turned her down flat because we wouldn't have a clue what it was worth or where to get rid of it."

"So what is it that you do, or did, with Johnnie?"

"You're no cop, right?"

I nodded, affecting my best non-cop face.

"Painkillers. OxyContin. Johnnie had a source. But she didn't want to sell it on the street. She knew we could get rid of it for her. That's it. Simple business deal."

"What was her source?"

He shrugged. "She mentioned some doctor, but not a name." He laughed. It was an off-putting laugh, derisive and singular. I was beginning to think that Jalil's assessment of his character was overly optimistic.

"Anyways, I don't know how she met the guy, but it wasn't too surprising. She had no problem with men. They had problems with her, though. She'd hook them, one way or the other. She had the looks, and she knew how to use 'em. I think she got some of them going online. She'd get 'em sending her money, promising goodies." He smiled or, more accurately, leered. "Don't know whether she found this doctor online or if he's here in the city somewhere. She was an ice princess man. Cold."

I assumed little Vince had struck out with her.

"Did she sell you a lot of OxyContin?"

"Pretty fair amount. It was regular. Every month."

"Was this just you and Scooter handling the trade or were the Blue Notes involved? Was Caballo Negro taking a cut of your action?"

He frowned, lowered his eyes, tightened his hands on the wheel. "This was our own thing."

"And Caballo was cool with that?"

Vince didn't answer, just stared out the window. I guessed Caballo would be none too pleased to find out that two of his soldiers were flexing their entrepreneurial muscles.

"Where'd you sell the Oxy?"

"Here and there."

A picture of Balboa High School in Mission Terrace popped into my mind. Painkillers were all too much the rage among San Francisco's teenagers. But solving that particular nasty wasn't on my agenda for today.

"What about the last time Johnnie came to see you?"

"What about it?"

"You cheated her out of some money. She was angry. What did you do to her?"

"Nothing. She blew off some steam. We had a little disagreement about one particular sale. It was a temporary issue. We weren't trying to screw her. Scooter had lost money he shouldn't have playing pool. We told her she'd get paid in a week, soon as we sold some more junk. She wasn't happy, but what was she gonna do?" He grinned, his mouth a lopsided insult.

"So she just left you guys, happy as a clam?"

"She was pissed. Said she'd only accept money in advance from then on. But she was okay with it. Nothing happened. She knew we'd pay up sooner or later."

"And that was the last time you saw her?"

"We didn't even know she'd disappeared till her little sister showed up and told us."

My blood started to heat up a little as I remembered the bruise on Frankie's arm. "Which one of you roughed her up?"

"Nobody. I mean, she went a little crazy and charged Scooter, and he grabbed her just so she wouldn't scratch his eyes out. It was self-defense. He didn't hurt her, really." Vince threw up his hands. I mean, whattaya gonna do? A little girl attacks you, all bets are off.

I examined him for a moment, then looked out the front toward Marsh's car. I thought Vince was telling me the truth. Mostly.

All else being equal, I tended to believe him about the artwork. It had never made any sense in terms of street value. Maybe Johnnie just told Frankie that it was the art that supported them, so she didn't have to tell her about the drugs. She probably just had a soft spot for art and indulged it when she could afford to. I couldn't tell about her taste—not that mine is refined or even roughly educated—because most of it had been destroyed by the intruder.

Whatever the whole truth, talking to Vince had only complicated matters. Now there was a supplier, a doctor if Vince was right. And other men, perhaps victims too, entangled with Johnnie.

Again, a scarecrow and a rooster loomed like a bad moon rising in my near future

CHAPTER 18

Maggie seemed a bit more clear-eyed, but also a touch sadder, not that she had seemed remotely happy before.

We were in Frankie's apartment, which, other than one lamp that had been placed back right side up, no one had bothered to clean up. Perhaps it was intentional, a signal to the little girl that if she showed up, there was nobody who cared a lick. Of course, no one had called the police. I had a feeling that even an on-premises murder wouldn't get Leonard or Maggie to call 911 if that meant a cop would step foot in the house.

Leonard wasn't home, and Maggie didn't know when he would be.

I didn't wait for Maggie to evidence signs of hospitality. I asked her if she had any coffee.

"Coffee? No." She frowned. "I mean. Yeah. Instant, I think."

"That'll be fine."

"Ah. Okay." She stood rooted in place, reflecting on my response, or wondering about why I was there, or considering the fact that it was well past the dawn of the new century and their household was perhaps the last in San Francisco still drinking instant coffee.

"I'd really appreciate it, Maggie. I didn't get much sleep last night." That wasn't really true, but little white lies are morally defensible.

"Uh huh." She waited a moment more and then slowly turned and scaled the stairs as if they were Mount Everest in a blizzard.

A few moments later, I found the key right where Frankie told me it would be, tucked in the top right-hand corner of the bookcase.

When things work out like that, all nice and neat and tidy, I start to worry because I'm always suspicious of easy solutions. I went to Johnnie's desk and, reaching under it, my spirits sank. The drawer was crooked, warped, the lock broken, the compartment empty.

I shook my head and cussed. Despite the fact that it confirmed my easy-peasy theory, it was frustrating, just like every other aspect of this case.

I was getting tired of it.

I looked around the room but saw no other hiding place that a computer might have taken up.

I stood there thinking until I heard Maggie's heavy footfalls on the stairs.

She handed me a blue mug full of black coffee. She hadn't asked my preferences regarding whiteners and sweeteners. I do prefer a dash of cream, and when I took a sip of the toxic instant brew, I winced.

Maggie stood back a few steps away from me and examined the floor.

"Sorry," she mumbled.

"About what?"

"Haven't had a chance to clean up down here." Her eyes stayed fixed on the underworld.

"Leonard called me."

That got her attention. She raised her eyes with a bewildered expression on her face.

"He said he doesn't want Frankie to come back here to her home. Wants to throw the little girl out on the street."

"Oh," Maggie sputtered. "That's not...he didn't mean—"

"He was pretty clear."

She closed her eyes and winced as if she had a headache. She wasn't beautiful or even pretty, but she had nice eyes, when they weren't lost in space, and a pleasant face that might be appealing if she could shake herself free of the robotic stupor.

When she opened her eyes, a transformation had occurred. A glint of determination. "Leonard cares too much about people. He doesn't want to hurt Frankie. I'm sure he's just concerned about us... about me," she said, with a slight blush. "What if whoever did this comes back? It's not safe for Frankie either. She should find another place where she could start over and forget the bad memories here."

"You talking about the break-in, or Johnnie's disappearance, or something else, Maggie?"

She looked like a deer caught in headlights for a moment, then blinked and said, "All that. It's so terrible about Johnnie, and it just doesn't look like she's going to...show up."

"Why don't you think so?"

"Because it's obvious she isn't, that's all," she hissed.

I was taken aback. This was the first time she'd evidenced the slightest anger, and it seemed totally inappropriate. "Why is that obvious? Is there something you haven't told me?"

The brief anger that had crossed her face morphed into something akin to mortification. "I don't know what...I'm sorry. I'm just frustrated, and I feel for Frankie. It's not fair what Johnnie did. The poor little girl has gone through so much." Maggie clasped her hands around her arms and hugged herself.

"I have a feeling you're not telling me everything, and I think it would be a good idea if you leveled with me now because—"

Upstairs the front door opened. "Maggie?" Leonard called out.

She gave me a lingering, pathetic look that implored me to be a good boy.

"We're down here, honey," she said, in that submissive tone that turned my stomach.

When Leonard joined us, pleasantries were not exchanged. As soon as he spotted me, he started right in. "Why are you back here? We have nothing to tell you. I thought I made myself clear."

He was wearing his usual attire—a Pendleton and dirty jeans. He'd added a black beret, angled to the right, trying to get the whole Continental thing going.

It wasn't working.

Some people rub you the wrong way. They may be perfectly nice, wonderful human beings. But something about their look or voice or syntax or overall presentation is just plain irritating.

Leonard had hit the trifecta with me. Although I'm sure he had his fine qualities, that I hadn't yet had the opportunity to discover, he was not a nice person. And he was one of the most annoying humans I'd ever met. He made me want to pull my hair out. Or, more precisely, his.

"You sure did, Len. Now, where's Johnnie's computer?"

"What are you talking about?"

I pointed at the desk. "This desk drawer was fine after the break-in. But somebody's jammed it open since then. This is where Johnnie kept her laptop locked away. Where is it?"

"I don't know what the fuck you're talking about."

Despite it all, I remained calm. "Do you like this look, Len?" I indicated our surroundings with a sweeping wave of my hand.

"What the hell?"

"Would you like your whole house re-decorated in this avant-garde style?"

His brow furrowed, his nose scrunched, the flesh of his cheeks tightened against his bones. Then, after a long moment, his eyes widened. "Now hold on here—"

"Where's the computer?"

"Fuck you."

"Okay. I'll start with your room."

I moved past him, and he made the mistake of attempting to stop me by grabbing my arm. Maggie cried out, and a moment later, from my position standing above his body on the floor, I said, "Do not ever touch me again."

He caught up with me when I'd found their bedroom, past two other small chambers, at the end of a long dingy hallway lit by a large glass bulb filled with dead insects and dust. He stood at the doorway, and Maggie, making bird-like tweets, rocked back and forth behind him as I began searching the room.

I'm not a fastidious man, but I threw caution to the wind and took no care at all with their belongings. I scoured the one wall length closet, tossing clothes and shoes over my shoulder. I picked up vintage *Playboys* and other nudie magazines on the floor of the closet and flung those into the bedroom.

"Goddammit," Leonard muttered over and over again.

I picked up a clock radio on the bedside table, yanked the cord out of the wall, dropped the musical timepiece on the floor. I searched under the mattress, peeked under the bed.

"I'm going to go and call the cops." He turned and stepped away, leaving Maggie hugging herself and impersonating a whip-poorwill.

"Please," she said. "Please, don't..."

It was so pitiful I almost stopped. But then I thought about Frankie.

I ripped the cover and sheets off the bed, overturned the mattress, catching a table lamp, which crashed to the floor and broke into pieces.

"Oh God," Maggie cried.

When I finished with the bedroom, it wasn't a pretty sight. But I have to admit, it wasn't in nearly as bad a condition as Frankie's apartment. Maggie stepped out of my way as I left the room. "What next?" I queried, to no one in particular.

When I got to the kitchen, Leonard was waiting for me. He was standing with his arms folded beside a cigarette-burned wood breakfast table that held a humongous candle half-melted down into a shape resembling Jabba the Hutt. Next to that was a dirty yellow vase containing a single plastic tulip. A cracked delft teapot sat on top of a stack of lined papers next to a tarnished silver laptop.

Leonard's eyes tracked mine to the computer.

"Are the cops on their way?"

He grimaced. "I forgot I even had the damn thing," he dared to mumble.

I lifted the computer lid and powered it on. It was a Mac Air, not too old, not too new, and there was not a damn thing on it. Not one file. From the looks of it, even the operating system did not exist.

I looked at Len. He smirked.

"You erased everything."

"I didn't do a damn thing to it. I found it that way."

"Why'd you take it at all?"

"I was trying to help—"

I laughed, or chuckled really. Couldn't help myself.

Len ignored me. "I figured there might be something on it that could maybe get us some information about where she was going that day or what she'd been doing..." He scratched his chin reflectively, trying to convince with dramatic concern.

"So you broke into her desk. You knew the computer was there."

"Yeah. I knew where she kept it. I don't remember how I found out, but I did. I figured it was worth breaking the lock to help Frankie find her sister."

Maggie appeared at the edge of the kitchen, her face a mask of fear and shame. She kept glancing up at Leonard and then quickly averted her gaze.

"I'm sorry, Len. I misjudged you. I guess you're just a good Samaritan, after all."

Leonard took the compliment in the spirit it was given. "Fuck you, Plank."

I folded the computer closed, picked it up, and headed for the exit.

"What are you doing? Jeez, you're a bastard. That isn't yours," Leonard called out after me.

Out on the porch, I drew a deep breath, trying to shake free of the sour stench of the house and the couple inside.

Maggie opened the front door, stepped onto the porch, and closed the door behind her. She reached up with both hands and grabbed the sides of her neck, rocking her head back and forth and side to side, a pained expression on her face.

"Mr. Plank, Max, I just...I wish. I forgot something. I should have told you before. It was just that..."

I waited. She dropped her hands limply to her sides, her head drooping down on her sloping shoulders. "Someone came by asking about Johnnie after she disappeared."

I wanted to be angry with her. I wanted to yell at her. I wanted to shake her. Instead, I just waited.

"He was nervous. He wanted to know where she was. How he could find her."

"Did he give a name?"

"No. He just said she didn't show up for a meeting and he was concerned about her. I told him that she hadn't been back to the house for almost a week and that I had no idea where she'd gone."

"What did he say to that?"

"He pressed me a little. Asked if I was sure. But, after a while, when he could see I didn't know anymore, he left." Once again, Maggie kept her eyes on the world beneath our feet.

"Could you describe him?"

"Maybe in his thirties. Black hair. He wore glasses. He was good-looking. Boyish. Well dressed. A suit and tie." She looked up at me for a brief moment to assess if she'd pleased me.

"Did you see a car? His car."

Her skin flushed while she looked straight into my eyes. "Yes. A Mercedes. Don't see many of those parked on this street. It was new. Black. When he left, I went to the front window and watched him drive away." She flashed a sly smile.

"You got the license plate." I was gobsmacked.

She reached into her pants pocket and handed me a piece of paper with four digits and three letters in the proper California license plate sequence. I stared down at the script for a few seconds.

"Why didn't you tell me before?"

"I didn't remember and...well, Leonard thought we shouldn't get involved. That it was too much of a risk. This man might be dangerous and he could come back. Please, Mr. Plank, if you find him, don't tell him how. Please."

The ripe smell of all the flowers on the porch was strong, along with that same underlying skunky marijuana scent. I couldn't imagine they were growing pot out here right at their front door, but maybe they had a medical license to do so. Either way, it was just one of the many mysteries at the heart of this couple and this house.

Of course, every couple, and every home has its mysteries.

I thought, for the umpteenth time since meeting him, of going back inside to administer a beating to Leonard but decided it wasn't worth bruising my knuckles and it wouldn't change anything anyway.

I asked Maggie if there was anything else she'd neglected to tell me and she promised that there wasn't. I didn't believe her, but I let it go. Against my better judgment and knowledge that it wasn't going to do a damn bit of good, I did give her my best advice.

"Maggie, you should leave Leonard. Get away now. As far as possible. Leave while you can."

She didn't answer, just stood there shaking her head from side to side, either saying no or I don't know. Maybe, she was saying, as so many desperate women before have said:

Are you kidding? Despite what you see, he's the love of my life. You don't know him like I know him.

I tucked the laptop under my right arm, the note with the license plate into my left pocket, and headed back down the stairs, hoping that this was my last trip here, but knowing deep down in my bones that it wouldn't be.

CHAPTER 19

"You want me to do what?"

Bo looked at me as if I had two heads.

"Good time to ask for a rent decrease."

Three heads now and a brain turned to marmalade.

"You've got to be kidding."

"I need a meeting. After my last visit to the casino, I don't want to tempt fate. And it'll take days to set something up if I do it his way. As his lessee, I know that you can reach him more quickly. Tell him it's important. Tell him to come on over tomorrow night for dinner. Tonight would be even better."

"Jeez, buddy, there's no telling what he'll think. He was just here. I have a number to a lawyer that handles his real estate stuff, I guess, but I've only called it once before."

Bo was looking sharp, in a black open-necked shirt and khaki pants, topping off brand new moccasins. He was looking thinner in just the past week. He told me he'd become a fruitarian a couple of weeks ago. He was mainly eating pineapple, mango, and flaxseed. I couldn't believe it would last, but it was definitely having an impact on his figure.

"Try. For me. Pretty please." I batted my eyelashes at him.

He sighed. "All right. But I don't have to have dinner with him and his posse again, right?"

"Nope. Just set up a time, and I'll take things from there."

"And you're not going to irritate him? I don't want him in my restaurant in a bad mood. That would not be good for business."

"*Moi?*" I said. "Since when have I irritated anyone?"

He gave me a look. I get that kind of look a lot from people who call themselves my friends. But a man's gotta do what a man's gotta do.

We were sitting at a table made of shiny metal in Rusty Root's large kitchen. The restaurant was still an hour from opening, but there was already all sorts of cutting and chopping and boiling and baking going on around us. Rope Rivers, his ever-present bandana around his forehead, was whistling Queen's, "We Are the Champions" while whisking a custard concoction that smelled of vanilla and licorice.

"Okay. I'll let you know if I get a response."

"*Danke.* How are the wedding plans coming along, Dad?"

"I don't know. Leaving that to the wife and daughter. I guess I should check in some time to make sure that I don't have to open another restaurant to pay for it."

I laughed, patted him on the back, and went out back to retrieve my Ducati. I had an appointment in Piedmont with a urologist. It seems that I suddenly suffered from an untimely bout of erectile dysfunction, and something about Dr. Stephen Wainright's license plate number, which I'd found through an online service that costs me under thirty bucks a month, told me that he was the man to help.

DR. WAINRIGHT'S OFFICES WERE LOCATED IN THE GLORIOUSLY exclusive upper crust hills of Piedmont, the toniest suburb this side of the Bay. It was surrounded by the messier, multi-ethnic diversity of Oakland, California, but nobody who lived there would readily admit that fact.

I pulled onto the tree-lined Grand Avenue near Piedmont's western border with Oakland and parked my bike across from a coffee and chocolate shop called Sweet Grounds, kitty corner to the doctor's place.

I sat on the bike for a moment, studying the lush environment. A lovely place to live and work, if you had the money. A small animal vibrated in my front pocket, and when I retrieved the phone, Marsh's mellifluous voice greeted me with his usual panache.

"Your girl likes art."

"Hello, Marsh."

"Portia has started restoring some files, and there are an awful lot that have to do with art and its attendant cornucopia."

I'd given Johnnie's computer to Marsh to see what could be recovered. Portia was Marsh's best computer mind. She used to be a hacker. Some would say she still is but receives a regular handsome check for it now. From what I could tell, her skill was extraordinary. Still, her name bothered me. So did her looks. With a name and a body like hers, she should be leading armies, breaking hearts, or slaying dragons—not playing with code. Maybe she did all those other things in her spare time.

"I believe you're taking liberties with that word."

"What word."

"The corn word."

"Nevertheless, she was deeply passionate about the art world."

"That's what she sold. It was her trade, I guess, more or less." Although it was becoming clear that that really wasn't the truth.

"More, I'd say. She didn't just sell it. It was more important to her than that."

Whatever that meant, I decided I could wait to find out. "What else has Portia found?"

"Nothing remarkable, but she's still looking. When she finishes the full restoration, there may be more."

"Good. Let me know."

He hung up without saying goodbye.

I dismounted my electric steed and marched toward my appointment with the urologist. Most men would be quite nervous before confronting another man about ED, but I was cool, calm, and seriously collected.

I SAT IN AN EXAMINATION OFFICE WONDERING WHY I'D CHOSEN ED as the malady to confront Dr. Wainright with. Perhaps my choice revealed an unconscious insecurity? Or was it the opposite side of the coin—a blustery machismo that feared nothing, least of all the dreaded ED.

The receptionist, a Ruben-esque middle-aged woman, oozed maternal vibes along with an unmistakable hint of wantonness in the hazel eyes. The nurse, a red-headed recent co-ed who cuffed me for blood pressure, slipped a digital thermometer delicately beneath my tongue, and asked me personal questions while glancing with what I thought was sympathy, but may have been pity, down at my file.

The pair were to ED as anti-venom is to a snake bite.

The good doctor left me twiddling my thumbs for almost twenty minutes. When he entered the room in his white robes and distracted friendliness, I was surprised (despite Maggie's semi-accurate description) to find a man both younger and more handsome than your average pledger to the Hippocratic oath. Younger than yours truly by several years and prettier than just about anybody outside of Hollywood's innermost sanctum.

I hadn't been to a doctor for a decade or more, and my memories of the trade arose primarily from my childhood when the most difficult feat was pretending that shots didn't bother me in the least. I loved the way Dr. Guadagni, after driving the needle deep into my anterior deltoid muscle, would tousle my hair, smile, glance at my mom, and say in that deep, doctorly voice, "He's a brave one," while I struggled not to grab my aching shoulder and cry out for my mommy.

So perhaps I can be forgiven for not knowing how best to conduct a dialogue with a medical professional.

"Mr...Plank?" he said, studying the clipboard dangling on his lap.

"Max," I said.

"So what brings you here today?"

A nice opening on his part. Let the patient do the heavy lifting. Speaking the words out loud might be the beginning of treatment. Should I say the words themselves, I can't get it up, or use the acronym, ED, to shorten the shame?

I decided on a wholly different tack.

"What can you tell me about Johnnie Damon?"

A long silence. I let it build.

Finally, a delayed and not-too-imaginative riposte. "What did you say?"

"Johnnie Damon. Twenty-two-year-old woman. Brown hair. Quite attractive. Lives with her little sister on Church Street across from Mission Dolores Park."

He looked into my eyes for a few seconds, and in that brief time, I saw his life flash before me. I knew just about everything I needed to, but not quite.

He dropped his gaze down to the clipboard where it stayed.

"Who are you?" he mumbled, without looking up.

"A friend of the little girl, Frankie. Maybe I can jog your memory a bit. You were at Johnnie and Frankie's house a couple of weeks ago. You talked to one of the landlords, Maggie. She remembers you and your car clearly. She said you were looking for Johnnie, that you were distressed about her disappearance."

The doctor took a long breath through his nose and looked into my eyes. "I don't have to talk to you."

"True. But I don't see why you wouldn't. A little girl has lost her sister, the only family she has. If you have any information at all, why wouldn't you want to help?"

He grimaced, paused, his features softening a bit. "It's not that I...I don't know anything. She was a patient. I don't know where she is and—"

"Hold on, Doc. Was she your patient? I don't know much about medicine and how it's practiced, but don't urologists deal with men's problems?"

He blinked three times. "I can't discuss her case."

I decided to let that go, even though it made no sense. "So you're in the habit of visiting patients at home on the spur of the moment?"

"We're finished," he said and stood up. "I guess you lied about your problem, so I'm going to ask you to leave right now and never come back."

I rose and got up close and personal with him. "Doctor, I know you were involved with her. If she was your patient, that isn't all she was to you. She's a missing person, and the police are going to be on the case soon. I'm going to be mentioning your name to them. And they're going to come see you. You might save yourself a lot of trouble if you just tell me what you know right now."

He took an awkward step back. "If you don't leave right now, I'm going to call..." His voice trailed off.

I turned away, opened the exam room door, and said over my shoulder, "I'll be seeing you real soon, Doc."

CHAPTER 20

Bo sat across from me in the bustling kitchen with a
stunned expression on his face.

"You could at least thank me," I said.

"Something's fishy." Bo shook his head in wonder.

"Don't look a gift-horse in the mouth, my friend."

"Don't mix metaphors, and what the hell does that mean,
anyway?"

I shrugged my shoulders.

"I still can't believe he lowered my rent ten percent. You
suggested it. You must have known something. But what could
you have on Poe that would make him do something so out of
character for him, or any other landlord I've had the misfortune
to encounter?"

I gave him an open-handed gesture, indicating my own cluelessness. I'd proposed it as a lark during our meeting at the casino
and was as shocked as Bo that Poe had actually remembered and
agreed to the request. Business at the restaurant was down a bit,
but nothing that couldn't be explained by seasonal variations and
the economy.

The unfathomable mysteries of Poe.

"Is he still in your office?"

Bo, still a little dazed, nodded. "He's only got one Neanderthal with him. He's expecting my return."

I rose and clapped Bo on the shoulder and said, "Thanks."

"Thanks to you, too, I guess. Although I'm not going to be surprised if this 'favor' comes back to haunt me. I can't imagine there won't be strings attached."

"O ye of little faith," I said and left him there to marvel at the perplexity of life itself.

POE SAT HUDDLED ON THE LEATHER COUCH WITH MY FRIEND REX, he of the visage only a mother could love, across from Bo's desk in the small, cluttered office. Several guitars were propped against the walls, which were lined with lots of black and white photos of San Francisco's music clubs and halls over the years.

Both Poe and Rex had iPads on their laps.

When I walked in, Poe looked up but displayed no overt surprise. At the same moment, Rex jumped to his feet and reached into his coat pocket. Poe stayed him with a raised hand. "Leave us alone. Stay close."

Rex shot me a less-than-fond expression but obeyed his boss, and five seconds later, Poe and I were alone together again. He wore his usual white shirt and black vest, sans sports coat.

"I thought I made it clear, Plank, I don't like surprise visits." His tone was measured, but you couldn't miss the hint of aggravation.

"I guess you won't buy that I was just visiting my friend, Bo, and he mentioned that you'd dropped by, and I thought it would be rude to leave without at least saying hello?"

He chuckled. It seemed a genuine chuckle, and once again, I thanked my lucky stars for my gift of amusing people. It is sometimes confused with annoying people, but you can't please everyone all the time.

"What do you want?" he said when he somehow quickly recovered from his mirth.

I leaned my butt back against Bo's desk and folded my arms across my chest. "I'm still trying to help the little girl, and it's been frustrating. Have you thought of anything else about Johnnie or the Blue Notes, or anything related that might help?"

Poe closed the lid on his iPad and laid it beside him, putting his hands together with his forefingers extended and touching his lips in a pensive motion. "I would have contacted you if there was anything to tell."

I pursed my lips and nodded. "Have you ever heard of a small time dealer by the name of Leonard Mackey?"

"Frankie and Johnnie's landlord, you mean?"

I was surprised, although I shouldn't have been, that he knew that little fact. "One and the same. I think he and his wife, Maggie, sell drugs and possibly more, to a local clientele. Strictly sleazy and small-time, from the looks of them."

Poe's tapped his fingers against his lips. Music, Vivaldi's *Four Seasons, Winter*, wafted into the room from someone's radio in the nearby kitchen. "He sells pot mostly, although when he can get his hands on crack or heroin or Oxy, he's not above taking that to the street."

"Women, too?" I asked.

Poe's eyebrows raised. Then he broke into a mischievous grin, and I knew what was coming. *"To be thoroughly conversant with a man's heart is to take our final lesson in the iron-clasped volume of despair."*

I smiled back at him. "Is that a yes via Edgar Allan?"

Poe re-steepled his fingers and said, "Let's just say that our Leonard dabbles in whatever trade will make his pockets jangle."

"Have you had dealings with him?"

Poe looked at me for a long time before answering. "This does not leave the room."

He waited until I nodded my assent.

"Art and Rex paid him a visit a few months back. Leonard was..." he reached behind his head and scratched his neck reflectively, "...getting involved in matters that were likely to get him into trouble."

"Involving Johnnie?"

"Obliquely."

"C'mon. Give me something."

"He'd somehow become cognizant of the fact that a certain local politician was involved in a potential conflict of interest, a brewing scandal, and he was concocting a blackmail scheme. Fortunately, he mentioned it to one of his drinking buddies, a contact of one of my associates, and we were able to nip it in the bud. For his own good, really, the man is not smart enough to pull off something like that."

"And how does Johnnie factor into this?"

"As I said, not directly. Just that Leonard was her landlord. That's about it."

That's about it.

Sure.

"Did your men rough him up?"

"They just talked to him, told him how inadvisable his plan was."

I'm sure they were a model of decorum. "And so he just dropped it?"

"Yes."

"No muss. No fuss."

"Something like that."

"I guess you're not going to tell me anything more about the politician or the scandal."

"Did I say scandal?"

"I must have misunderstood you."

"Yes, you must have."

"What else? How about the Blue Notes? Two of them bilked Johnnie out of some money. I guess they were doing street deals with her. I don't know what they were involved with. Frankie thinks her sister was peddling art to them wholesale, but they deny that. They say it was painkillers and the like. I think they're —at least the one I talked to—probably telling me the truth. But I can't be sure, and Johnnie isn't here to defend herself. Would you be able to exert any influence that might clarify what she was doing with these guys?"

Poe shook his head. "No."

"That's it?"

He glanced at the Rolex on his wrist, losing patience.

"One more question."

He sighed loudly, but I continued. "Do you know anything about a doctor by the name of Wainright? Operates out of Piedmont. A urologist."

"Never have had a need for that kind of service," he said flatly.

"And you know nothing about the man?"

He gave me an even look. "Why do you ask?"

"He was involved with Johnnie, too."

Poe's face remained noncommittal.

"I don't know exactly how yet, but I will. Something was going on between them. Whether it was intimacy or business, I don't know yet."

"Wainright, you say?"

I nodded.

The tip of his tongue peeked out between his teeth. "I can't help you."

"Okay. Thanks for your time and sorry for the interruption."

"Much as I enjoy these little chats, I hope this is the last time you surprise me."

I moved toward the door, but then turned back and said, "Why'd you lower Bo's rent?"

He smiled. "I'm not such a hard-hearted businessman. I want people to succeed. He's got a nice little place here. I like his food. If by giving up a little now, he can stay in business longer, and the people—" he waved his hand at an imaginary crowd of famished patrons, "—get the benefits of a fine restaurateur, then that's all to the good. No need to squeeze every last penny from good people."

I nodded and turned away, almost believing that he was sincere. Maybe he was, but I had a feeling, like Bo, that any favor now would inevitably lead to the future extraction of the proverbial pound of flesh.

CHAPTER 21

I'd never seen Portia wearing makeup, or dressed in the slightest bit of finery, or with her hair done in any remotely fashionable way.

She wore a black t-shirt and jeans. Both fit her body like handmade gloves. Her barely brushed blonde hair hung straight down to her shoulders. A half-dozen rings of varying sizes and patterns dangled from her voluptuous ears. I was sure there were more piercings hidden from view.

It didn't matter. She was a natural beauty with olive skin, big oval eyes, and an intensity of gaze that could weaken a strong man's knees.

I'm not mentioning names.

She had Johnnie's laptop open on the table in front of us and was explaining the various files she'd recovered.

We were on the third and top floor of Marsh's offices in Tiburon with its stunning views of Angel Island and the San Francisco skyline in the distance.

I'd driven across the Golden Gate because that's where Portia was and because it looked like I had another man, another possible suspect, to see in Sausalito. The more I found out about Johnnie, the wider and more tangled the web of mystery surrounding her seemed to get.

Portia had already shown me all the files and bookmarked sites and thousands of photos of artwork that Johnnie maintained. Most poignant was a file containing her resume and the many rejection slips she'd received from local art galleries where she'd applied for jobs. She had a decently written essay that emphasized her passion and knowledge about art and art history, but I noted that she was a high school dropout and figured that's why she couldn't get to first base with gallery owners.

The information on her computer made it clear that, whether she peddled art on the street or not, her love of it was unquestionable. She wrote about it in a diary she kept on her computer. She wrote with passion about her favorite artists and pieces with a sincerity and emotion that were almost too raw. It felt like a violation to be reading her private notes, and I didn't linger there.

"After reading this, I like her," Portia said. "Sure hope she's okay. I'd like to give her back her computer, face to face, maybe take her out for a cup of joe and a chat."

I nodded. "She was definitely crazy about art."

I thought about how this fit with the other people and aspects of the case but couldn't come to any particular conclusion.

"So where are the files that mention the doctor and the politician?"

She clicked the mouse and a folder labeled "Persistence of Memory" opened up. "She labeled this after a painting by Salvador Dali. I guess it's pretty famous," Portia said, glancing at me. She clicked again and a file opened with the painting. I hadn't known its title, but the painting was familiar. It is a surreal depiction of time with several melting pocket watches and a modern, bland, but strangely evocative seascape.

I stared at it for a moment, wondering what it had to do with Dr. Wainright and the politician.

Portia clicked on another file, and it opened a Word doc with half a page of notes. Stephen Wainright was printed at the top.

I scanned down the page, trying to make sense of the letters and numbers printed there. The information appeared to be in an improvised shorthand or code.

There were a few dates, running from about six months ago to the last one two weeks ago today. Next to those dates were numbers and letters: 24-O. 38-S. 60-P.

I stared at the data for a long time and then asked Portia to show me the politician's file.

Another click and the file opened above the other one.

The name Davis Hunter was highlighted at the top. Marsh had told me who the mystery pol was, but seeing it there in black and white still had its effect.

There was a little uptick in my heart's clicker rate.

Davis Hunter was the President of the San Francisco's Board of Supervisors.

The writing beneath his name was a little easier to figure out.

Unfortunately.

CHAPTER 22

D avis Hunter lived in an apartment on Nob Hill most of the week but appeared to often spend his weekends at a getaway in Sausalito, near the northern edge of the Golden Gate Bridge. It's another enclave of the monied atop a steep wooded hillside, overlooking the lively town and harbor, home to several houseboat communities. I knew a few of the guys who lived on the water and, once in a blue moon, attended parties there.

People who live on boats are as different as day and night, but they usually have a few things in common. One is a hatred of routines. And lawn. And staying put in one place, although many of them hardly ever move their boats. The possibility of movement is enough. Another is a wariness, a subtle suspicion of land lubbers. The feeling is probably mutual.

I knew no one living on the tony hill above, other than Davis Hunter, and I knew him by name and reputation only.

I took San Carlos Avenue and wound my way up the lush hillside, doubling back several times onto Spencer Avenue, until I passed Cloud View Park and Cloud View Road and arrived at Hunter's estate on, naturally, Cloud View Circle.

I don't use the word *estate* lightly. The thing sprawled like a wooly mammoth. Not to say it was covered in fur, but you somehow felt slightly diminished before its awesomeness. The edifice, a series of interwoven rectangular boxes constructed of stone and slate and marble, was set amidst a palette of soaring oaks, pines, and maples. Carefully tended bushes and giant plants guarded the entrance, all framed by a circular driveway.

I pulled up in front and sat on my bike for a few moments, taking in the breadth and width of the beast, breathing in the scents —the turpentine smell of the pines, a sweet floral orangey blush from nearby flowers, the slightest tang of sea salt in the breeze. While my nose was being tickled thusly, I considered my approach.

Davis Hunter owned a law firm whose offices took up two floors of a large building in the Embarcadero in San Francisco. He also developed real estate as a lucrative hobby. He had friends in high places and, no doubt, in low ones.

Johnnie's file on him revealed enough to more than limn the surface of their relationship, and a blush of the shady depths beneath.

I strolled to the massive teak front door and tapped a golden-hued knocker three times, stepped back, turned around, and waited.

A woman's laugh rang out from somewhere in the back of the house and then a shriek and the sound of splashing water.

I found a little doorbell ringer and leaned into it for a few seconds.

More laughter. More splashing.

It sounded like it was all happening in the backyard. I'd forgotten my swimsuit, but still, I didn't want to miss out on all the fun. I found a stone path on the side of the house and followed it through a narrow tunnel of trees and plants that brushed my body as I passed. The path ended at a white gate. I reached over the top and flipped the latch, which led me to be standing at the edge of a vast lawn fronted by an infinity pool and a stunning view looking out over Richardson Bay, the opposite peninsula containing Belvedere and Tiburon and Angel Island to the West.

A young, and quite naked, young woman with large breasts sat on the side of the pool with her feet dangling in the water. Davis Hunter snuggled next to her, fondling the breast closest to him and nuzzling the soft, white flesh at the nape of her neck.

I was about thirty yards from them, and at first, they didn't notice me. I couldn't blame them, caught up in what they were caught up in.

I cleared my throat and said, "Davis Hunter."

They both looked my way at the same time.

I waved in a friendly manner.

The woman said, "Shit," and dived into the pool.

Hunter stared at me for a few seconds, evidently debating whether or not I was a direct physical threat to him.

I held up my hands in what I thought was a peaceful gesture and didn't wait for him to formulate a question. "My name is Max Plank, and I need to talk with you. I'm sorry for showing up without an appointment, but it's very important and couldn't wait."

"Are you with the police? Do you have a warrant?"

Mmmm. Interesting questions. I shook my head in the negative.

"Then you're trespassing. You have no right to be here and—"

"I just need a few minutes of your time. After hearing me out, I'm sure you'll understand."

I had been walking slowly toward them and was no more than fifteen yards from the pool. Suntan lotion, chlorine, and sex sweat wafted in unequal proportions.

Hunter eyed me warily, sizing me up.

"Is this a legal problem? If so, please call my office during business hours, and I'm sure we'd be happy to..."

I shook my head causing his words to trail off. "It's a personal matter—"

"This is ridiculous. I won't allow—"

"I think you'll want to hear me out. It relates to you personally, Davis."

The woman's face bobbed near Hunter's feet in the water. She held onto the side of the pool with one hand while the other arm was wrapped around her chest. I wasn't peeking, but she wasn't buying it. "Davis," she said, her eyes big and fearful.

"Shhhh," he whispered to her, patting her on the head, and gave me a look that told me he was indisposed to grant my request.

"I know a reporter at the *Chronicle*. Maybe I'll take him to lunch. Or talk to Poe about you," I said with a shrug.

He stared at me with a look of consternation on his face for several long moments before I saw his expression break.

DAVIS HUNTER WAS IN HIS FIFTIES, IN GOOD SHAPE, WITH SHORT gray hair, cunning blue eyes, thin lips, a tiny nose, and big ears. He wasn't a handsome man, but he was neat and trim and vigorous looking.

We sat at the edge of his property in two blue Adirondack chairs looking out at the calm bay waters.

Katie, the young naked female, had been directed indoors by Hunter. I turned my back as she exited the pool, grabbed a towel, and pitter-pattered away.

"You embarrassed her," Davis said.

"She has nothing to be embarrassed about."

He frowned. "Are you a private investigator of some sort?

"Of some sort."

He gave me a funny look. I get that a lot.

"So what's this all about? I'm a busy man and—"

"I don't blame you. If I had Katie waiting, I'd be just as impatient."

He winced and looked at me like I was an alien from the Planet Asshole. "What'd you say your name was?"

"Plank. Max."

"Get on with it, Plank."

"I want to talk to you about your relationship with Johnnie Damon."

His glance flickered away. After a long pause, he stood up. He fixed me with a look that could kill and said, "Show yourself out."

"After you answer my questions."

"The police are right at the bottom of the hill. A phone call away."

"Comforting to know."

He spun on his heel and marched toward the house.

I called out to him. "Hear you don't mind the occasional golden shower, Hunter. And that's not the half of it, is it?"

That pulled him up short.

Really, I don't care what kind of so-called perversions a man has up his sleeve, long as he isn't hurting or taking advantage of somebody else. But enough was enough. It was time to figure out what the hell was going on in this confounding case. In general, I've found that people are inveterate prevaricators and liars, especially when it comes to their compulsions and private shames, and most particularly illegal ones, but everybody involved in this whole sordid affair was shut up as tight as an oyster tucked inside a clam buried a hundred feet below the bottom of the sea.

He didn't say a word, just turned and trudged back on over, settling himself slowly back down into that lovely chair right beside me.

Nothing like sharing intimacies to bring two men closer together.

After a good long while, he muttered, "What is it that you want?"

"I want to know what your relationship was, and is, with Johnnie."

"Does she have me on tape? Video?" He was looking out over the pool and the Bay, maybe searching for answers to the mystery of life out there, or more directly, wondering how much trouble or money his personal peccadillos were going to cost him.

I wasn't going to ease his mind. At least not until I got what I needed, and maybe not even then. Guys like Hunter bugged me. He was obviously an entitled son of a bitch. Maybe I was just jealous because I didn't have Katie drooling all over me.

"When was the last time you communicated with Johnnie?" I paused, following his eyes out to the great unknown beyond, and added, "And I need the truth. Don't try and lie to me because I've already talked to lots of people about her, including Poe, and I'll be able to tell if you're fibbing. If you start with that, then even a simpleton like me won't have too much trouble uploading some interesting media to the Internet."

Bullshit, yes. But what the hell. Remember what I said about those little white lies? Morally defensible and all.

He drew in the proverbial long breath followed by a truly exasperated sigh. Time passed. Finally, he managed, "I haven't spoken to her in more than two weeks."

"Can you give me an exact day or night?"

He crooked his mouth. "I think it was the tenth. A Wednesday night."

That meant he'd been thinking about that evening quite a bit. It was two days before Johnnie's disappearance. "Where'd you meet?"

He shuffled in his seat, rotated his head around on his shoulders, closed his eyes, tapped the chair with his fingers, turned, and gave me a look that managed to convey both bitterness and anger. "Can we cut to the chase here?"

"Nothing I'd like more. Let's do. Did you kill her?"

Another attention getter. His eyes widened. His hair stood on end. Okay, maybe I just imagined that part.

"Do you know who I am? You can't go around accusing a man like me of murder. Who the fuck do you think you are?"

Max Plank. That's my name and I'm sticking to it.

"You're married aren't you, Hunter?"

She was a socialite. She had more money than he did, and her contacts smoothed his way in business and politics. Her clan was one of the most hallowed of San Francisco's old families, dating back to the gold rush days. Her great, great grandfather had made his money bilking the hopeful fools panning for gold way back when. After that, they'd continued in the hospitality business and owned more than their fair share of the city's fine hotels and restaurants.

I had no idea how he could be so brazen with a girl like Katie here. Maybe his wife was too busy attending balls and ribbon cutting ceremonies to notice. Or maybe she was happy to have other women deal with his carnal desires. Maybe she had her own stream of young lovers.

The rich are not like you and me.

Well, I shouldn't speak for you.

"My marriage is none of your damn business."

"No, it isn't, you're right. But let's not kid anybody. Your bride might not care what the hell you're doing with Johnnie or the lovely Katie here..." I waved my hand in the general direction of the door in which she'd disappeared. At the same time—I'm ashamed to admit—briefly conjuring her comeliness.

"But the local reporters and pundits would be all too happy to make merry with mischief over these goings-on involving one of San Francisco's most storied families."

Daggers. Bullets. Flamethrowers.

Take your pick. Davis Hunter's eyes were shooting one or all of the above at yours truly.

After he finished giving me the evil eye, he looked away and opened up. "Look, sure. Johnnie and I were having an affair. I knew she was trouble, but...jeez, so seldom does one meet a woman so...skilled as her." He blushed. I was surprised to see it from such a worldly man. "I got a little carried away. I think I know what crack addicts must feel like. I couldn't get enough of her. And, believe it or not, Plank, I love her. Never felt anything like that before in my life."

I didn't say anything. True love can be hard to explain. I guess everybody has their version of it. I just don't think mine would include fucking someone like Kate within days of losing your one true love.

"I knew she needed help, too. She was involved with some bad people. I got an inkling of some of the shady activities she was involved with. She was dealing with street thugs. And Poe. I thought maybe I could help her out a little. I gave her some money. She had to hustle to support herself and that poor little girl. I tried to guide her along with the benefit of my advice."

I had a feeling that Johnnie had gotten far too much self-interested advice from too many powerful men.

"How'd you find out that she was missing?"

He closed his eyes. "It was crazy. We were supposed to meet. She'd never missed an appointment with me. She wasn't answering her phone. I was worried. So I called the landlord. A woman answered. Kind of a space cadet. I didn't say who I was. It was a little sketchy, but she told me that Johnnie had disappeared and mentioned the little girl was all alone." He shook his head from side to side.

So Maggie was still holding out on me. She was a space cadet. Perhaps her memory was foggy from all the drugs she'd obviously ingested.

"I went a little nuts, I guess. I spent some time outside her apartment, just watching. I never tried to go in. I didn't know what to do." He gave me a searching look. "I sure hope you can find her."

"How did you meet her?"

He looked out over the lawn, tapped his fingers against the chair and said, "A party out at Poe's casino a few months back. It was casual at first, we had some things in common. She loved art, and my wife's got a pretty extensive collection of moderns. She asked if there was any way she could see it."

It was an upscale variation on the hackneyed pickup line —*Young lady, would you like to come up to my garret and have a gander at my etchings?*

"Did you think of contacting Poe to see if he could help?"

"Thought about it. Thought better of it."

"So you confined your search for the woman you love to staring at her empty apartment?"

He gave me a foul look and said, "You don't understand."

"I'm just surprised, from what you tell me about the way you felt about her, and with your access to powerful people and resources, that you didn't try a little harder."

"Power, like all good things, comes with strings and limitations. But I'll have you know that I did get in touch with contacts at the SFPD, and they've been looking for her."

"Who in the department?"

"I'm not at liberty to say."

"I assume that, no matter what they find, they'll keep your name out of the paper."

"Of course. But I don't see that that matters."

Looked at in a less than flattering light, his reaching out to the police could be seen as self-serving. If a crime was involved, it was likely that the link from Johnnie to Hunter would be revealed. By contacting the cops, he was trying to eliminate the risk of them looking at him as a jilted lover and, therefore, a possible suspect. Might work, but probably not.

I handed him my card. "I want you to call me immediately if your contacts in the department give you any information. Anything at all. I mean it, Hunter."

He had a pained expression on his face but nodded his assent. "What about...the evidence...the video or whatever. Are you...?"

"You love her, but you think she taped your get togethers? You think she was going to blackmail you?"

His brow furrowed. "You said that..."

"You suggested it first. I was following your lead."

"So there aren't any tapes?"

"I didn't say that."

"What are you saying?"

"Not a damn thing. Have you told me everything you know about her disappearance? Is there anything you can think of that might help? Anything she said about the trouble she was in or somebody threatening her?"

"No. No. Nothing like that. I would have helped her if I thought she was in any kind of real danger."

I studied him for a moment. Maybe he would have done so. As long as it presented no danger to himself or his cushy life. Otherwise, he might just allow the nexus of his love addiction, with some regret, sure, to just fade away.

I told him that I might be back if I didn't hear from him.

"No. Don't come back here."

He offered his personal cell phone number, and I added it to my phone. I could wow my friends. The President of the Board of Supervisors and me, chummy as can be.

"I'll let you get back to it then," I said and headed back out the same way I came. As I crossed the lawn to the side of the house, I glanced back and caught Katie standing behind the glass patio doors in her teensy bikini staring at me with a disapproving expression on her face.

BEFORE LEAVING SAUSALITO, I STOPPED IN AT FRED'S COFFEE SHOP, a local institution, the bright yellow awning heralding its inception in 1966. It had been too long since I'd sampled their great French toast. My taste buds were talking, ignoring the long-term health of my vital organs.

I sat at a table out front, the deep fried French toast smothered in butter and syrup and sidled next to the seven-buck millionaire's bacon—thick slabs of sugared pork covered in red pepper flakes.

A young mother with three toddlers sat at a table nearby. The tykes were surprisingly well-behaved, each utterly involved with their pancakes and bacon. The little boy with a mop of flaming red hair wearing a contrasting blue jumpsuit leaned his head down beneath the table, tilted his plate, and let a pool of syrup run down into his mouth, over his chin, and onto his chest. "Robert," Mom said, although not harshly, but with an amused lilt in her voice. As she gently wiped the jumpsuit with her napkin, Robert blushed, righted his plate and, sighing, resigning himself to the indignity of manners, picked up his fork. Mama Bear was beatific, preternaturally calm, in her element.

I watched a steady stream of traffic on Bridgeway without seeing it, my mind busy sorting through and trying to make sense of the things I'd learned in the past few days.

One thing was certain. Johnnie had been involved with too many men. Men who were married. Maybe that had nothing to do with her disappearance, but somehow I doubted it.

Were Dr. Wainright or Davis Hunter guilty of anything other

than adultery? In Wainright's case, perhaps it was just a mid-life crisis, although if he'd been dealing painkillers through Johnnie, that was going to be another matter entirely. With Hunter, I gathered he and his wife were, at best, polyamorous, but more probably he'd just been cheating for a long time and she was the long-suffering wife. Maybe he had fallen hard for Johnnie, but he was a politician first and foremost, and therefore obsessed with appearances and PR.

Were either of these men capable of murder to protect their status, their positions, their families?

Of course. Anyone is capable, given the right circumstances and pressure, the perfect storm leading to an emotional breakdown.

Poe was capable of anything, but his connection was murky at best. Vince and Scooter were still primary suspects, no matter that I had a feeling that Vince had told me mostly the truth.

Leonard's connection to Johnnie had proved to be more complex and dicey than it first appeared. He probably was involved with her in questionable or illicit activities, and there was animosity between the two. And maybe more. Most men involved with Johnnie seemed to lose their bearings, to fall hard for her. Was Leonard just another one of those hapless males?

And did Maggie know anything about it?

I needed more.

I had to go see the urologist again. And a visit to Scooter was in the offing to see if he corroborated his partner's story.

As I picked up my cell phone to call Marsh, it vibrated in my hand.

The number looked familiar, but I didn't immediately identify it, not until I heard Maggie's voice sobbing into the phone.

CHAPTER 23

Back on that front porch, the smell of pot and flowers in my nose, I knocked on the front door.

After a few moments, I tried the knob, and it gave way.

Opening the door, I said, "Maggie?"

The house was alarmingly quiet.

"Maggie," I repeated.

My nose picked up the sickly sweet odor of decay.

"Max," Maggie muttered.

I followed the voice.

In the bedroom, she sat at the edge of the bed, her hands clasped in her lap, her eyes staring at the floor.

Leonard lay on top of the covers, his eyes closed, seemingly resting peacefully. The stench told another story.

I knelt at Maggie's feet and cupped my hands over hers. "When did you find him?"

It was a few minutes before 4 p.m.

Her face was red and puffy, stained with tears. There was a

catch in her throat when she answered me. "I...got back from the hairdresser about an hour ago."

"He was here, in bed?"

She nodded, not looking at me.

I rose and moved to Leonard. I checked his pulse. I felt his forehead. The stink rose, and my stomach churned. I put the back of my hand in front of my face and glanced at the bedside table.

A syringe, a spoon, a Q-tip, a lighter, and a small plastic bag with the remnants of a fine black grainy tar lay on the bedside table beside him.

I guess it wasn't too surprising, but for some reason, I didn't peg Leonard for a heroin addict.

"Have you called 911?"

She shook her head.

Why had she called me first? I suddenly felt terrible, realizing how sad it was that I was the first person she thought of calling.

I went to the kitchen and made the call, and when I returned, the drug paraphernalia on the table was gone.

I let it go. I'd tell one of the EMTs about the heroin.

Leonard didn't seem the type to kill himself: he was too self-involved. So that left an accidental overdose or maybe a heart problem exacerbated by drugs.

Unless somebody had killed him and made it look like the heroin did it.

Death, as life, is full of possibilities.

I DECIDED TO LEAVE BEFORE THE AUTHORITIES, THE COPS, AND ambulance showed up.

I left Maggie still sitting on the bed looking like a wispy tree in a hurricane, her hands clutching her body as if she was afraid it might fall apart if she let go.

She looked cadaverous.

For now, there was only the devastation of losing the most important person in the world. And I thought, at the time, that she might be too fragile, that her chances of survival seemed slim.

CHAPTER 24

That night, things started to go from bad to worse, the complexities and violence ratcheting up as if the probing and prodding I'd initiated had unleashed something hidden and dark and vengeful.

Frankie was spending the night with Dao and Meiying. They were going to make chicken fingers, Chinese style, whatever that might be, and then Dao promised to watch *Terminator 2* with her. She had to beg Meiying to watch, too, violent action flicks not being her thing. Meiying finally gave in as long as Frankie agreed to let her know when anything scary or violent happened so she could cover her eyes. Meiying was going to miss most of the movie.

I was sitting at my dinner table, finishing up the striper, sautéed with olives and capers, that I'd caught off the stern, savoring the tasty mix, which got me thinking about Katie, Hunter's little wench. Which got me thinking about Alexandra. Fortunately, my lascivious train of thoughts was interrupted by a call from Portia.

"I stumbled across another file on Johnnie's computer, and I thought it might be important."

"Hello, Portia."

"Yeah. So you told me how she had problems with these two guys from the Blue Notes?"

"Yup."

"She has a note about this guy, Scooter. She was really pissed at him. And she says that she's going to see CN. She knows that this will really upset Scooter, but she doesn't care. She says she told Scooter what she was going to do, and he threatened her. She wasn't worried about it because Scooter is a punk and a coward."

The lingering taste of the fish in my mouth tasted suddenly fishy. "Was this a file that you hadn't seen before or—"

"I missed it. It was a subfile, some notes hidden within another file. Kind of a journal. It ran to hundreds of pages over the past three or four years. I've skimmed most of it now, stumbled across this a little while ago. It looked like it might be important." She clucked twice, paused, clucked again.

It was definitely cluck-worthy information.

An hour later, two members of the San Francisco Police Department came knocking on my door. I let them in, and we gathered around my dinner table.

I figured it was a routine informational interview regarding Leonard's death.

"You like living on a boat, Mr. Plank?" One of the officers, a kid named Kurt, asked. He was young enough to be my son if I'd gotten married in high school, perish the thought.

"Suits me."

"It's always been a dream of mine," he said wistfully.

I nodded. Lots of people find it a romantic notion, but I find that for most, the reality is not so palatable.

That was all the young man said for a while as his partner, Pete, a cop in his fifties, took over. He was a stolid fellow with streaked brown hair, thick blue glasses, cauliflower ears, and a ruddy complexion.

He confirmed that I'd come to Maggie's house after she called me and that I'd seen Leonard's body and made the 911 call. He quizzed me about my involvement with the couple, and I told them as little as possible but indicated they were involved in a case I was working on. Pete asked me what case, and I shrugged my shoulders and told him I wasn't at liberty to disclose that information.

Pete didn't like that but didn't press it at that moment.

Then he shifted the questioning. "So could you tell where you were today, Mr. Plank?"

"I just told you I went to Maggie's after—"

"No. Before then. Where have you been all day?"

I believe I wrinkled my brow. "Why do you need to know that?"

"Can you just please answer the question?" he said.

"Nope."

"Nope?" Now his brow was wrinkled.

"Not until you tell me why."

Pete pursed his lips and nodded. "Did you recently threaten the deceased, Mr. Plank?"

Ah, now I got it. Maggie had fingered me. I was surprised, but shouldn't have been. In her emotional state, she might say anything.

"You'll have to speak with my attorney," I said. I'd had too much experience with cops and lawyers—and yes, even judges—over the years. I wasn't going to say another word to them.

Pete, I could tell, was getting a little pissed. His ruddy complexion darkened. He looked like a drinker and a smoker, and a taker of blood pressure medication.

His next question let me know that Maggie had completely thrown me under the bus. "Did you recently physically attack the deceased?"

Kurt acted like he wasn't even paying attention to our exchange. His eyes flitted about the cabin fondly, as if he couldn't wait to move right in.

"Sorry, officers, but I'm not going to answer any more questions without my attorney."

"Shame. We could have cleared this up quickly. No muss. No fuss. But now, Mr. Plank, you've complicated things."

"What makes you think the deceased was murdered?" I asked.

"Nothing. We don't have a cause of death. The coroner's report is still out. We're working on the assumption that it was a drug overdose," Pete said.

"I don't get it."

"We have an obligation to the victim and to the spouse, sir. Your questionable, and quite possibly illegal, behavior toward her husband has to be investigated. The cause of death may seem obvious, but it might have been planned to look that way. In any case, you will have to answer these allegations sooner or later."

I nodded. I grabbed my wallet off a table, fished out a card, and handed it to Pete.

The card had Marsh Chapin's name on it. He was my attorney, just as he was my best friend, my partner, my financial advisor, and my trainer.

The cop glanced at it, grunted, shoved it in his pocket.

"Let's go, Kurt," he said and turned away.

Kurt smiled, took one long last lingering look around my boat, and reluctantly followed.

CHAPTER 25

I had a hard time getting to sleep that night.

And it wasn't because I had any worry about being a suspect in Leonard's death.

Nor was I worried about why Maggie had so willingly implicated me in the matter. I thought she'd probably volunteered the information about my less than amicable relationship with her lover because the police probably hadn't questioned her too hard, not at least until they got the coroner's report back.

Well, that did bug me a little. I thought there was some sympathy between us, but I guessed I was wrong. Perhaps she was just emotionally disheveled and didn't think through what the possible effect of her words would have. Or maybe she really thought that somehow I'd been responsible for Leonard's death.

I thought about it for a while but came to no conclusion. I wanted to pay her another visit and try to sort things out, but, all things considered, realized that probably wasn't a good idea.

There was an almost full moon visible through the porthole above my bed, and I reflected upon it, wondering what in the heavens was wrong with people, particularly the people I'd met in this case.

Once again, I tried to make sense of all the various threads spinning out from one little girl's dilemma. Once again, I got no closer to clarity.

I'd called Marsh after the cops' visit, but he hadn't answered his phone. I remembered something about a special evening that Tom had planned. Was that tonight?

I needed Marsh's aid, not only to deal with the authorities, but also to help me with the home invasion I was planning.

CHAPTER 26

In the morning, sipping coffee on my deck beneath a brooding gray sky, still unable to rouse Marsh (maybe Tom had kidnapped him and was holding him in captivity until he agreed to get married?), I decided to hold off on the home invasion for one more day.

Instead, I was going to simply invade someone's privacy and, hopefully, force them into telling me the truth.

I called Meiying to ask after Frankie, and she said that the little girl was using the boat as a skateboard park, which made Dao a little nervous, but other than that, they loved the kid.

I asked if they could keep her for a couple more days, and she seemed delighted. She wanted to take Frankie to the Exploratorium in the Embarcadero, then to Chinatown for lunch, and on to one of the big fish aquarium vendors in the neighborhood. Dao and Meiying had a 150-gallon saltwater tank embedded in a wall in the main galley of their boat.

After I hung up, I worried for a moment that Meiying was going to be heartsick when the little girl went away.

A moment was all I had, though, and soon I was back on the

Ducati with the wind in my hair, crossing the Bay Bridge towards Oakland.

IT WAS SATURDAY, SO I ASSUMED I MIGHT MORE LIKELY FIND DR. Wainright at his home in the Montclair hills, rather than his posh office in Piedmont.

He lived in the heavily wooded area below Highway 13, comfortably sheltered from the traffic noise.

I drove up a long, winding, tree-lined driveway about a hundred yards before I encountered the house, a sprawling California redwood contemporary home. Nothing compared to Davis Hunter's Sausalito digs, but impressive nevertheless.

I rang the bell once and waited, looking around. There were lots of trees and bushes, rocks and larger boulders, and plantings made to look like nature, wild and haphazard. But the human hand was evident in the meticulous presentation.

The front door swung open, and a woman in her thirties faced me with a questioning look.

"Hello," she said.

She was beautiful and she was sick.

The skin on her face was tight against the high cheekbones. Her pallor extreme, her eyes sunken into her skull. Her blonde hair was tied back in a tight bun. Her arms were thin twigs, the thickness of an adolescent.

She smiled at me, and it was a lovely smile, despite what was eating her alive.

I tried to smile back, but don't know if I managed it, as I suddenly felt sick, too. I didn't want to be there anymore.

"Can I help you?" she said. Her voice was thin and hoarse.

"Is Dr. Wainright home?" My voice was gentle.

"Who are you?" she asked, without a hint of fear or anxiety. She seemed calm, placid, despite it all.

"An old friend....from school. High school. I'm sorry, I was in the area and realized...remembered that he lived here and...I know it's a bit rude to show up like this, but I haven't seen him for a very long time and was hoping..." I let my words trail off.

"You attended St. Ignatius?" she asked.

I nodded, embarrassed. The Jesuit-run college prep is well known in the area.

She gave me a steady look, sizing me up.

"All right, Mr...?"

"Plank. Max Plank."

"Paul is out in the backyard gardening. C'mon in."

She led me through a front hall that had walls covered with family photos. The two of them on bicycles and beaches and mountains and trails, often with big wide smiles, often holding hands, or hugging each other.

We passed through a kitchen replete with the usual stainless steel appliances and black granite countertops. She opened French doors, and we stepped out onto a brick patio. The yard was a beautifully maintained amalgam of green lawn, brick planters, and bright flowerbeds.

Wainright had a shovel in his hand and was digging around in an enclosed vegetable garden.

"Steve," she called out, and her voice broke. She cleared her throat.

He looked up, resting his hands on the top of the shovel. When his eyes fell on me, his face darkened.

"This is Max Plank, your friend from Saint Ignatius?" she said with a question in her tone.

He stared at me for a moment and then his eyes closed with a look of resignation.

"You do know him, don't you, sweetheart?" A note of alarm rose in her voice for the first time.

He opened his eyes and managed a smile. "Yes, of course. Good to see you again, Max."

I nodded.

She relaxed.

"Well, I'm afraid I'm a bit tired. I'll leave you two to catch up." She turned, then turned back. "Is there anything I can get you, Max? Coffee, tea?"

I shook my head. "No. Thanks very much."

She smiled again, although it was tinged with pain now, and left us.

WE SAT IN THE MIDDLE OF THE GARDEN ON A BLACK STEEL BENCH with a wooden seat covered with vinyl cushions, as Wainright spilled his guts.

"...I was desperate. I didn't care what trouble I got in afterward. I only cared about saving Katherine."

He closed his eyes, clasped his hands, and brought the tips of his fingers against his nose. "There was nothing I wouldn't do...do you understand? Right or wrong was meaningless. If I lost her, I wouldn't have anything anyway. I was crazy. I still am."

I just let him talk. I'd come here ready to blow the man's life up if necessary to get at the truth, only to find out his life was already in shambles.

"I've loved her since the first time I saw her. We were first-year students at Berkeley, both taking an astronomy class. The feeling never wavered, not once in fifteen years. That's the truth. I know what they say about relationships and marriage, the work it takes to keep things going, the ups and downs. That didn't happen to us. We couldn't have kids. I couldn't. She was okay with that. She said I was all she needed. That's all I ever cared about—making her happy, taking care of her." His voice wavered, and he took a breath to calm himself. "We were always just...right for each other.

I don't know how unusual it is, but I thank God every day for her."
He paused again, winced. "At least when I'm not cursing Him for
her illness."

"What does she have?"

"Cancer. Pancreatic. By the time she was diagnosed, it was
Exocrine Stage Four, with the worst prognosis."

"I'm sorry."

"There was an experimental treatment that showed some
success with mice. But she didn't qualify for it because of her stag-
ing. The drugs cost hundreds of thousands of dollars. We had no
money. I'd lost most of it when the market crashed in 2008. I
couldn't accept that. If there was any possibility of her living, for
even just a few more months, I wasn't going to let her go."

"So what did you do?"

"I found Johnnie Damon."

"How?"

"Online. A forum. For OxyContin users."

"You're kidding?"

"No. I'd already decided that I might be able to make a lot of
money fast by selling the stuff. I didn't have the kind of patients
generally who needed painkillers, but I knew there was an
epidemic. I started doing research. I knew some doctors who
were enmeshed in the problem, trying to help the profession deal
with the fallout and the political ramifications." Wainright stared
straight ahead, tapping his nose with his fingertips, his voice flat.
"One of them told me about this forum as a way of describing
how tough the problem was. He mentioned that there are secret
forums for all kinds of things where people encourage other
people in the most destructive behaviors, including drug abuse
and suicide."

And I thought Internet porn was a problem.

Wainright continued. "This site was a way for sellers to meet
buyers and vice versa. It took some time for me to get accepted as

legit. But I was relentless, and the administrators eventually let me play.

"At first, I was clueless, fumbling around, not knowing how to approach people. Who to trust. After a few days of bumbling, I ran into Johnnie online and we clicked. Wasn't long before I agreed to meet her in person."

"Where?"

"A bar in Berkeley."

"What happened?"

He stopped tapping his fingers and looked at me. "She was looking for Oxy. Lots of it. She told me her story. I told her mine. I don't think there was any pretense between us. I don't know...she wasn't what I expected, not that I have any experience with drug dealers."

"What do you mean?"

"She was smart. Very smart. She was just a kid, really. In her early twenties. Trying to deal with the bad hand life had dealt her. Losing her parents. Trying to take care of her kid sister."

"Doesn't explain why she turned to selling drugs...or hustling men."

He gave me a surprised look. "She didn't try to hustle me. I got the feeling that she'd tried to find other ways to make money but couldn't. She'd had to drop out of high school. The cost of living around here is ridiculous. She was fearful of losing her sister."

Wainright gripped his knees and said, "Anyway, we kind of trusted each other. She was always straight with me. Telling me exactly how much I would make from each delivery and then getting me the money on time."

"Didn't you have to be careful?"

"Sure. And I was. But maybe not as careful as I should have been. Like I said, I was crazy, and the danger to me was less important than getting Katherine the help she needed."

"Did she?"

He shook his head sadly. "She got through the first round of treatments. But they didn't work. No remission. Not even a short one."

"But she's still alive."

He nodded, then looked up into my eyes. "For a little while longer. She's strong. God, is she tough. The doctors are amazed. But it's only a matter of time, and there's not much left."

I nodded, stayed quiet.

"So you never had an affair with Johnnie? It was strictly business?"

"No. An affair? Never," he snapped.

"When was the last time you saw her? The last time you sold her stuff?"

"About three weeks ago. I'd raised enough money for the first round of treatments but thought I'd need more for the next rounds. Since then, we've found out they didn't work. But when she didn't respond to my messages, I went to her apartment. I don't know what I was doing. I talked to her landlord." He turned to me. "I'm sorry about her disappearance. I hope she's okay. I liked her."

"Did she ever mention anything to you about her business or personal problems? Anyone who was threatening her or who she was afraid of? Anything like that?"

"No. Nothing. We were cordial. She asked about my wife. I asked about her sister, but she never went into any detail about her personal problems."

He rose, grabbed the shovel, and stood with his back to me. "So, what now?" he said.

"I don't know," I said.

He tapped the tip of the shovel against the soil several times, making a shushing sound. "Are you going to turn me in?"

"If what you told me is the whole truth, then no. I only want to help Frankie find her sister. What you did was wrong. But that's between you, your wife, and your maker. I won't judge it. I might have done the same thing in your place."

"My wife doesn't know anything about this. She would never have let me put myself at risk."

"She sounds like a good woman. I could tell...just looking at her."

"She..." Tears filled his eyes, and he turned away.

"Okay," I mumbled, and feeling more than a little shame tinged with sorrow, left him there alone.

CHAPTER 27

M arsh had finally surfaced.
But he didn't want to talk about where he'd
been, or how he and Tom were doing, or any other
thing that bordered on the personal.

Just Marsh being Marsh.

When I told him about the home invasion, he got really
excited.

CABALLO NEGRO HAD DINNER WITH HIS GRANDMOTHER EVERY
Friday night without fail and usually spent the night in a spare
bedroom.

Marsh had paid a follow-up visit to Vince, who, although
initially reticent to cooperate, had soon found himself eager to
provide salient details about his scary ass boss's life.

I guess a scary ass in the hand is worth two in the bush.

By the time we got there, it was just after 9 p.m., and the
streets were deserted, windswept, dark as ink. The moon was a
pale sickle in the murky sky.

The house was an old Victorian on Mason Street, a stone's throw from the famous Painted Ladies on Alamo Square—a tight ladder of Victorians, back-dropped by skyscrapers that tourists flocked to ogle.

Caballo had purchased the house for his grandmother a year ago for just under two-million dollars. He was doing quite well for a lad of twenty-seven, putting the lie to the aphorism that crime doesn't pay.

Caballo seemed to be mimicking the Hollywood cliché about gang leaders with a soft spot for family and, especially, the dear old Grandmother who raised him. They were probably having homemade apple pie for dessert. It was almost heart-warming.

But cornering Caballo at his other haunts—his high-rise condo downtown or Funky Jack's—presented loads more problems, as he employed Fort Knox level security systems and armed guards.

Here, other than a couple of his bored foot soldiers posted outside, there appeared to be little interference.

Of course, we guessed there might be more of his friends inside and that he would never be far from a weapon, no matter how safe he felt in the warmth of his grandmother's embrace.

From another of Marsh's cars, a black BMW not sold in the U.S., we watched the men at the front of the house for a while, recognizing one of them from our visit to Funky Jack's. After studying their lack of movement for about ten minutes, we formulated an impromptu plan, and Marsh gathered appropriate supplies from a satchel he'd tossed into the back seat.

I jumped a wooden fence into the small backyard and made my way toward the front of the house via a weathered brick pathway through a nice vegetable garden, from which I plucked a ripe red strawberry. Marsh headed up Mason, passing the house from the opposite side of the street.

Frank, the plump Mexican who'd made the mistake of

attacking Marsh with a knife, was smoking a cigarette and leaning against one of the concrete pillars holding up the front porch of Grandmother Caballo's handsome house. The other guard, also puffing away, stood back near the elegantly trimmed front door.

When the street was clear of pedestrians, Marsh came out of the shadows up the street and walked into the reflection of the streetlight in front of the house, strolling like any other passerby. Frank glanced at him briefly but didn't pay him any mind as he approached the steps leading to the porch.

Suddenly, Marsh pivoted, leaped the stairs, and landed within a couple of feet of Frank, who stumbled back, reaching too late inside his trench coat. Marsh's hand beat his to the gun. Frank's eyes became saucers as his mouth flew open to shout. But before he could manage that, Marsh shoved a tennis ball in it and kneed him in the groin.

Frank collapsed to his knees. Marsh slammed the side of his fist beneath the man's ear, and he toppled over unconscious.

The other guard would have reacted decisively if he hadn't simultaneously been upended into a rhododendron. After I'd opened a side gate and managed to nestle myself quietly behind the rhodie, I waited until Marsh engaged Frank. The man was standing near enough to the edge of the porch that I was able to grab his ankles and yank them and his legs out from under him. He hit the concrete porch face first with a bone-crunching thud. I dragged him off the landing and into said flowering plant. He was already groggy so, with a shuddering of leaves, I made him less alert, and then quickly bound his hands behind him. I gagged him with one of Marsh's tennis balls and used masking tape to prevent him from spitting it out. I left him hidden beneath the big plant.

Marsh completed the same procedure with Frank and dumped him into the thick shrubbery on the other side of the porch.

The whole procedure took less than a minute and, we hoped, was quiet enough not to alert the occupants.

The Victorian had a nice, newly repaired brick chimney jutting out of the spanking new roof, and we thought about surprising everybody by slithering down it Santa style, but it wasn't anywhere near Christmas, so we decided on the direct approach.

That might be even more surprising.

I put on a yellow overcoat with stripes and a cool red cap that had SFPD printed on it. I'd wanted an ax, but Marsh had nixed the idea.

The front door had lights on either side and a peeper smack dab in the center. I used the lovely brass knocker and tapped it firmly three times. Marsh moved out of eyeshot.

I heard some steps nearing the door and then sensed someone watching me through the peephole.

"Who is it?" a gruff voice asked.

"Fire Department," I said, in my best no-nonsense manner.

"What do you want?"

I thought that was a little impertinent. "Open up, please. There's a gas leak in the system, and we have to check out your main."

"I don't understand."

He would soon.

"Sir, please open up. It won't take long, but there are fire and explosion dangers to the house and yourselves."

Several locks were fiddled with and a chain unfastened before the door opened and I was confronted by a man of large proportions with an obviously bad temperament. He appeared weaponless, but I had no doubt that armaments were hidden nearby.

He scowled at me and said, "This isn't a good time. Couldn't you come back in the morning?"

"The danger is now, sir. How many people are in the house?"

"Me and my boss and his grandmother."

"That's all?"

He nodded.

"What's going on, Del?" The voice was resonant, commanding, with a slight Hispanic accent.

A moment later, the owner of the voice strolled into the picture.

Caballo was bald, wiry, riddled with tattoos, and had an unpleasant face despite its attractive individual features: high cheekbones, strong aquiline nose, full lips. On somebody else, these would have made the man almost pretty, but there was something in his dark blue eyes that drew you to them instead.

I guess you couldn't afford to be too cute if you had a mob that you had to keep in fear and in thrall.

"You're with the fire department?" he asked, squinting at me.

I lowered my head and stepped inside. Marsh was right behind me.

"Where's your furnace?" I asked authoritatively.

"Wait a sec...I know you..." Caballo was still giving me the eagle eye.

Del stepped behind the door. I looked at Marsh, who was already on the move.

Caballo reached behind his back. I stepped inside his legs, grabbed his elbow, and whispered, "We just want to talk. No threat."

"You're the fuckers who beat up my men at Funky's. This is not cool, man. Is my grandmama's home," he spat through clenched teeth.

"Just a few questions and then we'll leave you alone."

"Ernie, is something wrong?"

An old woman using a cane appeared in the hallway. She was probably in her eighties, almost as bald as Caballo, with rheumy eyes and an alarmed expression on her face as she studied the scene in front of her.

Caballo relaxed, and I stepped away.

"No, Abuelita. Just a little misunderstanding. Go back in the kitchen, and I'll be in to make your dessert in a few minutes."

The old woman's teeth chattered, and there were spasms in her face muscles. "Del," Caballo barked, "could you help her back and wait for me there."

Del, an abashed look on his face, as I assume Marsh had prevented him from retrieving his weapon, stepped from behind the open front door and escorted Granny away.

Caballo motioned with his head towards a large living area to the side. As he turned, I noticed the knife in its sheath at his back.

"THAT'S MY BUSINESS," CABALLO SAID WITH HIS HANDS GRIPPING HIS knees.

He was sitting on the edge of an upholstered chair in the center of the room. Marsh and I sat on identical love seats opposite each other, framing the leader of the Blue Notes. The living room was decorated in a distinctly Edwardian style with lots of excessive and unnecessary flourishes, including the pictures on the walls and the area rug depicting scenes from fox hunts.

Grandmama looked more Mexican than British, but it's everyone's right to construct their own narratives.

"We're just looking for the girl. She's been missing for weeks now and her baby sister is all alone. We're not trying to implicate you in anything, just trying to locate her. It's our understanding that she came to see you about a week before she disappeared because she was unhappy about a deal, a problem she had with some of your men."

Caballo shrugged his shoulders, shooting us a who-gives-a-horse's-ass look.

Marsh stood up and did a backbend, a forward bend, and then jumped into a handstand.

Caballo looked at him as if a llama had suddenly appeared in the room.

"Marsh," I said, with a hint of warning in my voice.

"We do need to know what she told you," Marsh said from his upside down position.

Caballo stared at Marsh, who started walking in a circle. A headstand circle.

"What the hell is he doing, man?" Caballo asked me.

"I don't think he had time to work on his practice today. He hates to miss a day. Then again," I added.

Suddenly, Marsh somersaulted, landing on his feet in front of Caballo, who showed the reflexes of a cat, leaping up onto his chair, reaching behind for the knife. But he was too slow. Marsh slashed at his wrist; the knife clattered to the floor.

Marsh started doing toe dips, up and down. Up and down. His eyes fixed on Caballo.

Who looked to me for help.

I shrugged. "Marsh doesn't have my patience. He wants to get home. He likes to meditate at night before sleep."

"Where the fuck are you guys from?" Caballo said. He was still standing on his chair. I could see he was trying to figure out his next move, but Marsh had thrown him off his game.

I could empathize.

"I told you that I never discuss my business with outsiders. Not phony firemen. Not cops. Not nobody. Now I'm going back to the kitchen to eat some of my Abuelita's flan. You guys can stay here and stand on your fucking heads all night, but I'd like you to get the hell out of my fucking house."

He stepped off the chair and endeavored to circumvent Marsh, but instead found himself seated stiff as a board with a pronounced wince on his face. Marsh was behind him, applying force to the young tough's shoulders.

Caballo closed his eyes and tried to bite back the pain, but it was only a matter of time as Marsh tightened his grip on the scapular muscles.

Unfortunately, for him and others unlucky enough to raise Marsh's ire, my friend has a surgeon's knowledge of human anatomy and physiology but had forsworn the Hippocratic oath.

"Caballo, your secrets are safe with us. We have no current interest in your organization's activities. But we won't leave here until you tell us what Johnnie talked to you about."

"Man..." he grunted. "Fuckin' shit, dammit, that...okay...okay...let up...let up...okay."

Marsh let his hands linger for a few more seconds before pulling away, but remained poised behind the chair.

Caballo grabbed his shoulders and tried to rub out the hurt. "Jesus and Mary!" he grunted, shaking his head. He looked like he was trying not to cry.

"Tell me. And it had better be the truth because I'll know if it's not."

He closed his eyes for a few seconds, shaking his head as if he could not believe what was happening. He opened his eyes and stared at me for a long time before saying, "You guys don't know who you're messing with."

Marsh smiled. I kept a straight face and said nothing.

"You're making me violate a core principle, man," Caballo said.

A moral dilemma, to be sure, for a paragon like him. Once again I said, "Just between us. Like I said. Whatever you tell me."

He nodded, scowled, then told us what we wanted to know.

It wasn't easy listening, but after hearing him out, I felt like there might be the slightest glimmer of light at the end of the dark tunnel we'd been stumbling through.

CHAPTER 28

Alexandra arrived on a red eye, and I was waiting at American's baggage claim for her at 7 a.m.

She grumbled about the fact that they'd forced her to check her carry-on luggage and complained about how the rack used to measure acceptable size seemed to get smaller every time she flew. She said the food, what there was of it, sucked, too.

She was tired and grumpy. And cute. Very cute.

I nodded sympathetically but couldn't take my eyes off her face. If we weren't walking through a major airport, I wouldn't have taken my hands off her body either.

I knew I should end it with her. She was different than any other woman I'd ever been close to, but that didn't make me different. I was the same old bastard. It was only a matter of time until she recognized it.

I knew it wouldn't last. It couldn't. With me, these things never do.

On the ride back to her place, she told me about her trip and the progress of the case she was working on. It was a nasty piece of business involving the international sex trade with tentacles spreading from Kazakhstan to Thailand to the American heart-land. She'd interviewed social workers and activists and, most importantly, gotten a lead involving a mysterious man who was working for immigration services and was supposedly the ring-leader of the whole dark operation. But the name she had didn't link up with anyone she could find, at least not yet. She'd put out a bunch of feelers to her network worldwide and was waiting impatiently for someone to provide the next clue.

I told her how Frankie and Johnnie's case was just about as frustrating as hers, although, with Caballo's information, there was at least a semi-clear path forward.

She told me to be careful, that I was involved with powerful people and that when powerful people were threatened, things could get ugly.

I didn't have to tell her that I did ugly pretty well and that Marsh fit ugly like a velvet glove. Still, I took her point.

I reminded her about the street fair Meiying had invited her to later in the day. She promised she'd be there, but she was exhausted, and by the time we got home, I reluctantly tucked her into bed and kissed her goodnight.

I MET MARSH BACK AT HIS NORTH BEACH OFFICE OFF COLUMBUS Avenue, the heart of the Italian-Chinese nexus of the city.

His office overlooked Washington Square Park, which fronted Saint Peter and Paul's church where I'd been baptized—and where Marilyn Monroe married Joe DiMaggio, mere feet from where the priest splashed holy water all over my face.

You draw the parallels.

Marsh sat in his high-backed leather recliner, and I lounged on a cushiony couch nearby.

His office was minimalist in decor. White walls with pristine white carpet. Black and white photos of martial artists, some of them Marsh himself, flying through the air with the greatest of ease.

"So who do we pay a visit to first?" Marsh raised an eyebrow.

"Has to be Davis."

"I agree. I don't even want to think about our approach to Poe."

"He's next, though. Doubt there's any way around it."

Marsh sighed. "Not if you insist on seeing this case to the end."

I gave him a look.

He nodded. He knew me better than anyone, and my sorry tendency toward dogged persistence was a personality defect he'd given up trying to change.

"Still, let's see what Davis tells us before we rattle Poe's cage."

"Let's start thinking of an approach."

Marsh pursed his lips. "Okay. But, you know, even if you survive the initial encounter, your life expectancy might be significantly shortened if we cross Poe the wrong way."

"I'd say both of us," I responded with as cheerful a voice as I could manage.

"As long as we've got that straight."

I LEFT MARSH TO FINALIZE DETAILS OF OUR IMPENDING VISIT WITH the President of the San Francisco Board of Supervisors and headed back to my boat to check up on Frankie and Meiying and Alexandra, who were all supposed to be together at a street festival at Fisherman's Wharf later in the day.

It was 2 p.m., and I thought Alexandra wouldn't join the ladies until at least 4 p.m., so I stopped at a library to use the computers for research about San Francisco city government. When that was finished, I had a quick meal of veal piccata and Swiss chard at the 622 Club.

By the time I made it down to the festival, it was after 4:30

p.m. I found them, sticky-faced with cotton candy, in front of Madame Tussaud's Wax Museum.

I got my face a little sticky, too, and then we wandered around for a couple of hours watching street performers—jugglers, face-painters, aerialists, jokesters, singers, dancers, and other assorted minstrels—and getting a big kick out of Frankie's wide-eyed appreciation of it all. At one point, she actually drew a little crowd herself, performing amazing feats on that skateboard of hers.

Finally, Meiying tired and invited us all back to her boat for dinner, promising that Dao would prepare us something special.

I told the women to go ahead, that I needed to stop by my houseboat for a change of shoes and a shower.

IT WAS PAST TWILIGHT WHEN I STEPPED ON THE GANGPLANK FROM the pier to my boat. The sky was moonless and dark.

I smelled barbecue chicken and coffee wafting over from my neighbors' boats.

My mind was occupied with riddles involving Frankie and Johnnie, and Davis and Poe, and the Blue Notes. And also, in the background, my strong but conflicted feelings about what I should do with Alexandra. How long I could let it go on intensifying, how unfair that was to her and...

And that's why I was not as attuned to my surroundings as I usually am.

The first intimations of something not quite right hit me as I placed a foot on the stairs leading down to the cabin. But it was too late by then.

At the sounds of something moving swiftly behind me, I turned, bringing up my arm, but a moment later, I shuddered, my head smashed, ringing, the shimmering lights of surrounding boats extinguished, my legs collapsing.

I tumbled, end over end, into oblivion.

CHAPTER 29

The first thing I became aware of as I regained consciousness was that I was being French kissed.

This did not seem, at first, entirely unpleasant, but soon the feeling was spoiled by my realization that I was being tongued by a cat.

I recoiled, grabbed Red with shaky hands, and moved him away. He meowed in irritation or satisfaction, I was too groggy to tell which.

The French kissing diverted my attention from Barry Manilow.

His voice sailing along in the night air, singing about writing the songs that make the whole world sing.

For a long time, until I actually read the lyrics, I thought that Barry was being just a tad arrogant.

My perspective was hazy, but with a little time, I was able to verify that I was lying on the floor of my cabin. I sat up and grabbed the back of my head. It hurt like the dickens. There was a concussion-worthy lump there on the right side. I winced, groaned, snarled a little, maybe, and looked up into Scooter's eyes.

Behind him, Vince paced nervously. Next to him Del stood strong and stoic.

Two other men lurked in the shadows near the stairwell.

I rubbed my bump, glared, and remained quiet.

"You shouldna' gone to Caballo's Grandmama's house, man. That wasn't a nice thing to do," Del said.

"Not smart neither," Scooter added. "First you come crashing into our clubhouse, you and that maniac friend of yours, and then you make a disturbance at Grandmama's house. Ain't you got no consideration for nothing, man?"

"You forgot something else."

Scooter gave me a questioning look. "Did you tell him about our little talk, Vince?"

Vince stopped pacing and gave me a look of disbelief. He actually blushed.

I continued. "Vince and I had a nice, long talk about how you two had a side business with Johnnie, cutting your boss Caballo out of the action. Does he know what you two bad boys have been up to?"

Scooter leaned forward and slapped me hard across the face. My head rocked to the side, my headache trebled in pain. I believe I growled, trying not to cry out.

"What's he talking about, Vince?" Del asked, furrowing that Neanderthal brow.

Scooter turned and flashed a dirty look at Vince, who looked away sheepishly. "Nuthin'," he said. "Asshole's a liar. Caballo knows everything."

I decided not to pursue the point at that very moment because I didn't think my brain could take anymore jostling.

Del nodded. I knew that Caballo knew all about what Scooter and Vince had been up to. I also knew Scooter and Vince didn't know about Johnnie's visit to their boss, so it provided a little leverage, or, I hoped it might.

I gritted my teeth and looked at Scooter. I wasn't restrained in any way, which was a mistake on the boys' part, but I had to consider there were five of them, and they were armed.

I had to keep them talking until I gathered my wits and strength.

"What's the plan, guys?" I asked as politely as I could manage.

The answer to my question surprised the holy heck out of me.

"Where's the computer?" Del asked.

"What are you talking about?" It wasn't hard to project befuddlement.

"Johnnie's laptop computer. We want it."

I studied Del's face, which was impassive, then Scooter's smirk.

"Johnnie's computer," I repeated, stalling for time. "Now what would you guys...what would Caballo want with that?"

"None of your fucking ass business," Scooter said, leaning in toward me again. He curled his hand into a fist and raised it. I bounced on my butt back as far as I could get and feinted with my head. He grinned at me.

"Just give it to us and you'll only get a beating," Del said. "Otherwise, things might get a little unpleasant. Trust me, man, got some guys here who love to wreak havoc."

Wreak havoc?

My god, they were children.

My head still hurt like hell, but the world around me was now sharper, crisper, the sights and sounds real again. I scanned my enemies and my houseboat for options. None immediately presented themselves.

"I don't have Johnnie's laptop."

"Don't lie to us, man. We know you do. We know you took it from her house. Leonard told us."

I guess it wasn't a shock that Leonard and the Blue Notes's

paths had crossed, but how closely had he been working with them? And how closely with Johnnie?

"Leonard's dead," I said.

No one burst into tears at the news.

"Did you kill him?" I asked.

"We're wasting time," Del said, moving toward me while calling out to the men behind him, "Zack, Marco."

I scrambled on the floor toward the corner of the room, raising my hands up. "Hold on, boys. Hold on. I didn't say I didn't know where it is, just that I don't have it right here."

Del stopped a few feet away and glared down at me expectantly.

"Okay if I get up?" I asked.

He nodded. Scooter removed a handgun from inside the leather jacket he was wearing and pointed it at me. One of the men near the door leveled a sawed-off shotgun at me. The other moved his hand inside his jacket. Vince just took a step back and continued to look like he'd rather be anywhere on Earth but right here.

I stumbled to my feet, and my head started swimming. I closed my eyes, opened them, and felt dizzy for a few more seconds before settling down. I was nauseous, and the pain hadn't eased at all. I put my hand down on one of the breakfast table chairs to steady myself.

I rubbed my sweat-stained forehead with my other hand and mumbled weakly, "Leonard wiped the computer clean. I would guess he told you that. I took it to a computer whiz, but she hasn't been able to restore the hard drive."

"Where is it?"

"At her office."

"The address, man. Are you dense or just acting that way?"

A little of both. I gave them the address.

"So it's there now? The office is closed, right? You have a key?"

I shrugged. He took a warning step toward me.

"Yeah. We can get in."

"Okay. Let's go."

Scooter and Vince moved forward and took my arms. I didn't think the time or situation was right to resist. I let them drag me outside, followed by Del and Zack and Marco.

CHAPTER 30

I soon found myself in the back of a beat-up Chevy van along with Scooter and Vince and Del, while Zack drove and Marco rode shotgun, literally, next to him.

The seats had been pulled out of the van, and it was just a big empty, ugly, shag carpeted space. I was propped near the right rear hubcap, and the others stationed themselves roughly at the other three wheels.

The van reeked of man sweat and cigarette smoke. Marco calmly smoked while Vince nervously tugged on nicotine-soaked paper.

There wasn't any chit chat on our fifteen-minute ride up toward North Beach.

They were all the strong, silent type, although I had my doubts about Vince.

We parked near Washington Square Park and were surprised by all the activity. There was a big crowd milling about and lots of couples and families set up on chairs and blankets on the sprawling lawn. A gigantic screen in the middle of the park was playing a movie—Meg Ryan and Billy Crystal looming large.

"For chrissakes, what's this, Plank?" Del said.

"Looks like it's Film Night in the Park. Have you seen *When Harry Met Sally*, Del?"

"Is this some trick, cuz if you're trying—"

"Yeah. Sure. I set the whole thing up. Planned for your visit, talked the city authorities into the movie. Just so I could get you guys here to see a romantic comedy to warm the cockles of your hearts."

"Smart guy," Scooter said and gave me another sharp rap on my skull.

I winced, growled again. I was coming to dislike the boy immensely.

"No funny business," Del reiterated.

Before we left the safety of the van, he peppered me with questions and warnings about what to expect. He asked me if anyone else would be in the office at this time of night. He asked me where Marsh was. He warned me what would happen if I tried anything or if I signaled anyone in any way as to the reality of the situation. He told me what would happen unless they left with the computer.

I gave him answers and reassured him about my honorable intentions.

They made sure I saw the automatic pistols that they all carried beneath their coats.

Vince and Marco stayed in the car, and Del, Scooter, and Zack escorted me to the lobby door. I pressed a button, and the security guard let us in. His name was Winston. He was in his fifties, a former horse jockey, small but compact, although he'd gained a few pounds since his riding days at Bay Meadows and Golden Gate Fields.

He smiled when he saw me but gave my friends the once over good.

I reassured him. "These are friends of my younger brother, Dave. We were out tonight, and I promised I'd show them the offices. We won't be long." I touched his hand tenderly.

I turned away and marched toward the elevator with my compatriots close behind.

UP ON THE SIXTH FLOOR, I SWITCHED ON THE OVERHEAD LIGHTS and led them to Marsh's office at the back of the building. From there, we looked down on the crowd and the big movie screen. Meg Ryan was about to fake an orgasm in a coffee shop to prove to Billy Crystal that he couldn't tell the difference between the real thing and the fake one. If you're of the male persuasion, it is a profoundly disturbing performance on Meg's part.

I stood there watching until Del said, "Where the hell is the computer?"

"Oh...yes. This is such a good movie, guys. If you haven't seen it, now's your chance. It'll make your hearts break and then soar."

"Fuckin' a hole," Vince sneered.

Unfortunately, he was one of those guys without a romantic bone in his body.

"All right, fellas. So I think she was working on it in the conference room over there." I pointed with my thumb back toward the middle of the web of offices.

"Then why the fuck did you bring us here?" Del asked.

"Look at that view down there. I mean, I know you guys mean business, but there's always time to appreciate beauty, natural and man-made, no?"

Scooter took another swing at me, but I ducked in time. I pivoted, reacting instinctively, but I heard the click of a bullet sliding into Zack's automatic pistol and instead paused and placed both my feet back down. Del and Zack both had their guns pointed at me.

I raised my hands up in surrender. "Okay. Okay. Let's go get it then."

I strolled out of Marsh's office wondering where the hell I was going to go next.

I TURNED LEFT AT THE CONFERENCE ROOM.

The main table, a great big gleaming mahogany thing that was rarely used, had nothing at all on its surface.

I stopped, frowned. Looked back at my captors. "It was here last time I saw it. She was working on it right at this table."

Del and Scooter stepped toward me. I danced away. "Wait a minute, guys. It has to be here. No reason it wouldn't be. It's probably in one of the other offices. We'll just have to search them."

Del narrowed his gaze on mine. "Whose offices are these anyway?"

"Marsh's. The computer whiz works for him."

"And where is he now?"

I shrugged.

"Let's go. Right now. We've already wasted too much time. You'd better find that computer, and fast, or that bump on your head is going to be the least of your problems," Del said.

I moved around him, avoided Scooter's reach, and headed to the next office.

IT'S TOO BAD THAT MARSH'S OFFICES WEREN'T AS BIG AS, LET'S SAY, the headquarters for Exxon Mobil. Then I might have been able to stall all night. As it was, there were only eight offices, and despite as much lingering as I felt the situation could bear, we arrived at the final office a mere ten minutes later.

As we crossed the threshold, Del said, "This is not looking good. Particularly, for you. That computer had better be here or..."

"Or what, Delly boy?"

Talk about warming the cockles of your heart, that voice certainly did the trick for me.

As we all turned to see who the strange speaker was, all hell broke loose.

Only one shot was fired, by Zack, and that one took out a few ceiling tiles, exploding papery debris all over everybody like it was New Year's Eve.

I took out Scooter's legs immediately after Marsh spoke. A moment later, after the kick to Zack's midsection that fueled the errant bullet, Del was grunting and pleading beneath a painful headlock. Marsh had kicked Zack's gun to the corner and was standing on his chest while I had my foot on Scooter's throat. He gurgled for breath beneath me but, remembering his smacks to my head, for the first few seconds, I showed no mercy and didn't let up until his face started to turn purple.

When I did lift my foot, he rolled over and retched onto the hardwood floor.

CHAPTER 31

"Winston," I said to Marsh. He nodded, and at the same time, reached into Del's jacket and removed his gun. He handed it to me.

"Good man," I responded when he was done.

"That's why I employ him."

"What do you want to do with them?"

"Any of these windows open?"

"Unfortunately, not."

"I think their heads might be hard enough to break the glass. At least, it's worth a try." With my foot on the back of Scooter's skull, I fumbled inside his coat and found his pistol.

"Might take a while to break through the double glaze."

"I've got time. There are two more outside waiting in a van."

"Want me to go get them?"

"Sure. One's got a sawed-off shotgun."

Marsh nodded, picked up Zack's gun, and handed it to me. He let go of Del, who dropped out of the headlock and made a big dull thumping sound when his body hit the floor. Marsh left us without another word.

I stepped back and motioned with a gun in each hand for the boys to gather themselves together in a corner of the room. They gave me dirty, pained looks but obeyed.

MARSH RETURNED TEN MINUTES LATER WITH VINCE AND MARCO.

Both men looked chastened, although to be honest, Vince had looked that way since I saw him on my boat.

We zip-tied the boys' hands behind their backs, marched them into the conference room, and sat them down in chairs on one side of the mahogany table, facing Marsh and me.

They were a sorry sight, but I didn't feel sorry for them. I touched my big bump and grimaced before starting. "So tell me why Caballo wants Johnnie's computer?"

I had my guesses, but I wanted to be sure.

I looked at Del, who was the leader of this bunch and, I was sure, the closest to the boss.

He shook his head. He gave me a look that indicated he'd just as soon bite off my hand as answer my question.

"You two are really in trouble, but you're too stupid to realize it. Give us the laptop and let us go, and I'll put in a good word for you." I had to give it to Del, he was a true believer in the power and glory of his boss. I wish I had a couple of minions like him at my beck and call.

I looked at Marsh. "Maybe we'd better do as he says."

"It would be prudent, I'm sure."

We both turned our eyes back to Del.

"A good word with Caballo, you mean?"

It was then that I saw something in his eyes and knew I had it all wrong.

AFTER WE ESCORTED THE BOYS BACK TO THEIR VAN, FREED THEM from the zip-ties, and bid them *adieu* without their weapons, I asked Marsh if he'd decided where best to confront Davis Hunter.

He nodded. We watched the van until its taillights disappeared behind the church, and then I turned and my eyes fell back on the huge screen. The audience was quiet as Meg Ryan and Billy Crystal stared at each other, realizing the truth of what we'd known for the past ninety plus minutes.

My cell phone jangled me out of the moment, and I reached in my pocket and took it out.

Alexandra's soft voice rang in my ear.

"Honey, what happened? Where are you? I've been so worried..."

CHAPTER 32

A couple of days later, I was wondering what was taking Marsh so long to get back to me with the plans for Davis Hunter, and, especially, our approach to Poe.

He'd made himself scarce again but assured me he was in the process of scouting and planning. The man had access to people, power, and logistical support that dwarfed any mere mortal's attempt at subterfuge.

I was a little worried that Caballo's men might make another run at us, this time with greater numbers, but thought they'd lick their wounds and bide their time.

Of course, it depended on how desperate they were to get their hands on Johnnie's computer. If, as I suspected, it wasn't Caballo himself after the laptop, then the danger and unpredictability factor was greater.

In the meantime, all I could do was keep my eyes open and my senses on alert. I was spending a lot of time with Alexandra, who was spending a lot of time with Frankie.

We'd taken her to Golden Gate Park and the Steinhart Aquarium, which I'd loved as a kid. It had been remodeled and lost some of the dark, subterranean feel—the wow factor tinged with a little danger that had sparked my imagination so many years ago. But it had gained a lot in size and fish. Seeing it again through Frankie's eyes was a kick. We also took her to the zoo, the latest Pixar movie, and a picnic in Tiburon.

It felt like we were a family, which made me nervous, despite the fact that I enjoyed myself more than I wanted to admit.

ON FRIDAY NIGHT, FRANKIE WAS HAVING DINNER AND THEN BINGE-watching *Arrow* on the *Sweet and Sour* with Meiying and Dao while Alexandra and I were alone in her cozy place in Pacific Heights.

We were sitting on the couch in the living room, thigh to thigh, drinking Cabernet and waiting for a pizza to be delivered. Alexandra was obsessing about the difficulties with her global slave trade investigation. She'd interviewed several women and young girls who'd been enmeshed in sexual slavery before managing to escape or being freed by activists in Thailand or Bosnia. There was a look of anguish on her face as she described the degradations that the women, some of them as young as nine years old, had suffered.

"So we have a guy at the magazine combing the Dark Web for us..." She paused, gnawing at a fingernail, shaking her head. "Max, you wouldn't believe some of the stuff on there. And the perverts and creeps and sadists who prowl those hidden alleys. Pedophiles and assassins and terrorists and drug runners all seem to play with impunity there."

Using TOR's network and its virtual tunnels, Marsh had once given me a brief tour and explanation of the Dark Web, which pretty much confirmed what Alexandra was saying, although there were also more innocent pastimes going on in that hidden realm.

"Problem is, Jasper—that's the *Independent's* hacker—while he's nibbled around the edges of the ring, hasn't been able to penetrate it to any great extent. The contacts he's met online are wary, and there are layers of protective walls around the information we need. There seems to be a hub right here in San Francisco, but we haven't been able to penetrate that link at all.

"Maybe I could convince Marsh to let Portia take a look at it."

"You said she's really good, right? So's Jasper but...I'm ready to let someone else have a crack at it."

Marsh maintained that there weren't more than a dozen hackers in the world with Portia's skills, and I'd seen nothing to doubt that.

"I'll talk to Harold and see if he's willing to pay for outside help, and then you can go to Portia." Alexandra took a sip of wine, resting the glass against her lips, staring at the fireplace mantle.

"If he says no, she might do it for free, although that's against Marsh's religion. She's pretty fierce when it comes to women's issues, and Marsh has been known to sin occasionally."

The doorbell rang. I could already smell the anchovies and garlic and banana peppers covering the best damn crust in the city courtesy of Palio's Pizzeria.

LATER THAT NIGHT, I WAS SOUND ASLEEP, NAKED, WITH THE equally naked Alexandra Stone snoozing against my chest, when the phone rang.

Still in my birthday suit, I stumbled into the kitchen and grabbed the offending receiver.

"We're all set. Get dressed and meet me outside, pronto. Rock 'n roll tonight."

The phone clicked off. I hadn't said a word or acknowledged him in any way. Maybe he could tell it was me by the sound of my breathing?

I PEEKED THROUGH THE LIVING ROOM BLINDS, AND SURE ENOUGH, Marsh was parked in front of the house in a sleek, black BMW, the engine purring like a cat.

I went back to the bedroom and informed my groggy girl that I had to go with Marsh but told her to go back to sleep and I'd call her in the morning.

She groaned and whispered, "Okay, sweetie. Be careful." She kissed my lips.

Reluctantly, I pulled away from her, got un-naked, and slipped quietly out the door to join my crazy ass friend.

CHAPTER 33

As we drove, Marsh explained his urgency.
"We can kill two birds with one stone for one night only."

He was dressed in his version of combat fatigues—black from head to toe. He had a matching uniform for me, along with a bagful of tricks in a satchel resting on the back seat, including two .22 caliber Berettas.

He knew I didn't like guns and only employed them in emergencies, but he assured me this was exactly that, if I considered imminent death an emergency.

He'd trained me a couple years back, and I practiced on his personal shooting range fairly regularly. I was comfortable shooting, if not carrying the damn things.

"The birds you mean are Davis and Poe?"

He nodded and shifted into fourth gear as we hit the 101 highway heading south.

"They're together?" I asked, having a hard time believing that might be true and that Marsh had divined the meeting in advance.

"Very hush hush, of course. The President of the San Francisco

Board of Supervisors can't be seen consorting with a guy like Poe, despite the fact he brings in more tax revenues than any other major San Francisco corporation. Most citizens probably figure Hunter and Poe know each other, but neither of them wants to be seen being chummy on the front page of the *Examiner*."

"How'd you find out about this meeting?"

"Pretty easy, really, after you gave me his private cell phone number. Portia had no trouble hacking into it and, for now, we have a live feed. I think you panicked Hunter with your surprise visit. It still took him a couple of days to get through to Poe, but when he did, he said some awfully disparaging things about you."

"You can't please all the people all—"

"He's afraid that you've got a video or some other kind of evidence about his kinky preferences and his involvement with Johnnie, and that you might use it to ruin him. Anyway, listen to this."

Marsh clicked on a file with a music symbol, and a man's agitated voice trembled out...

"...YOU SAID IF I COOPERATED THAT NOTHING WOULD EVER COME OUT. Well, if this jerkoff Plank goes to the press and has evidence of me and Johnnie, all hell's going to break loose. And believe me, Poe, I'm not going down alone. You introduced me to her for chrissakes. My conduct and votes on the board are going to be examined. The approvals we pushed through for you...look, I'm not—

"Be very careful, Hunter."

THE VOICE WAS FOREBODING AND UNMISTAKABLY POE.

"DON'T THREATEN ME. THIS IS GOING TO RUIN MY CAREER AND

marriage. You have to do something. Man like you should be able to take care of this two-bit detective."

"Two-bit," I said.

Marsh clicked off the recording. "I don't think that comment is the most important one on the tape."

"Easy for you to say. What if I called you a two-bit hustler or a two-bit trader or a two-bit builder or..."

Marsh rolled his eyes and clicked on the audio again.

"Did he say he had evidence and that he was going to use it?" Poe asked in an even tone.

A woman's sultry voice called out Hunter's name, and he told her he'd be out in a minute. The sound of papers shuffling and then he continued.

"Not exactly. He said he had evidence. He knew things. Things he could learn only by a hidden camera or if Johnnie talked to him directly, which is unlikely. He threatened to expose me on the Internet or to the cops, but then he indicated that as long as I was cooperative in his attempts to find Johnnie, he'd hold off."

"So nothing to worry about for the moment."

"That's not good enough. I can't wait for the the other shoe to drop. I'm President of the Board. You promised to protect me and I expect you to keep your word. This will hurt you too...I mean it..."

HIS PITIFUL VOICE TRAILED OFF. IT SOUNDED LIKE HE MIGHT START sobbing.

There was a long silence and then Poe spoke.

"ALL RIGHT. COME AND SEE ME TONIGHT. THE STORAGE BUILDING, OUT near the army barracks. You've been there. Meet me at 12:30 a.m."

"Why?"

"I DON'T HAVE ANY MORE TIME TO TALK RIGHT NOW. WE NEED TO HASH things out between us, and face to face is best. Then we can decide what to do with this detective bothering you. And let's just make sure we're both on the same page, comfortable with each other, moving forward."

"But—"

"Tonight, Hunter."

POE HUNG UP, AND THE RECORDING ENDED.

"Well, how about that," I marveled.

"A surprising turn of events," Marsh said.

"That Poe would talk on a cell phone and allow Hunter to say what he said?"

"Yes. He's too smart for that. Either he's getting fat and sloppy with his success, or something else is going on."

"So Poe played matchmaker for Hunter and Johnnie. Do you think he may have used that to leverage favorable actions and votes to get his casino approvals?"

"If I had a million dollars to spare, I'd wager a yes," I said.

"If I were Davis, I'd be very careful this evening."

"I don't think Poe would risk murdering a politician so prominent, not with the possible trails leading back to him."

"You never know. At heart, Poe is a dangerous jackal. His unpredictability is part and parcel of his success. Maybe he intends to off Davis and figures he'll have his cell phone with him so he can destroy that, and any potential evidence, at the same time."

"Seems too risky."

"For you, yes. For a man like Poe who, perhaps, is feeling pretty invulnerable, it might just be another day at the office."

WE WERE ON 80 NOW, HEADING ACROSS THE BAY BRIDGE TOWARD Treasure Island.

There was electricity in the air. I saw a flash of lightening in the distance over the east bay. Ten seconds later, the boom of thunder reached our ears. A few seconds later, raindrops began streaking the windshield.

It was 11:55 p.m. The plan was to arrive shortly after the meeting was scheduled to begin, giving the boys time to exchange niceties and settle in comfortably.

As we approached the Treasure Island exit off the bridge, Marsh explained his hastily drawn up approach, which included a great deal of improvisation.

Nothing too unusual. Kept things exciting.

CHAPTER 34

The building that Poe designated for the meeting was a couple of blocks behind the Island's Pier 1 and the Sailing Center, down an unpaved road right next to some old Army barracks.

Marsh had already used Google Maps to check the area out, and his plan was to approach the industrial building from behind the barracks where we left his car. He fished zip-ties, a small but powerful flashlight, some rope, a lock gun, and extra .22 rounds and tucked them into a fanny pack.

He handed me a holster and gun, and I clasped it together over my shoulder. He tossed me sleek synthetic gloves and put on a pair of his own.

It was raining pretty heavily, and Marsh, ever prepared, donned a black rain slicker stored in his trunk and shoved another into my hands.

Lightning streaked the sky in the distance, crackling thunder accompanied within milliseconds, and dark pudgy clouds above us rained down their contents, making the slickers slicker.

We crossed a large barren field full of weeds, rocks, tumbling paper, Styrofoam cups, and candy wrappers caught up in the windy gusts.

When we flattened our backs against the back wall of the building, it was 12:42 a.m.

We hadn't noticed any other cars parked nearby.

Poe had specified that the meeting was going to take place in a room in the southeastern corner of the building and that Davis could enter from unlocked double doors at the north entrance. Lights in the lobby and the stairwell would be on, and he was to climb to the second floor for the rendezvous.

We found the designated entrance, and the double doors, solid slabs of cheap wood, were still open.

But there were no lights on in the lobby, or from all appearances, anywhere in the building.

Marsh switched on the flashlight, and we examined the room.

Which wasn't a lobby, but a large storage space with a single unadorned lightbulb in the ceiling and boxes stacked high on all four walls.

The boxes had labels indicating that they contained soda pop and plastic cups and napkins and straws and after that, I stopped examining them.

Just plain old storage for the casino's many restaurants and bars.

A crash of thunder landed seemingly right outside the door, and the whole room shook for a moment. A jolt of sympathetic electricity ran up my legs.

"Wowee," I whispered.

Marsh frowned at me and said, "Hard to imagine Hunter Davis being comfortable coming to this place alone at this time of night."

I agreed and wondered if he'd chickened out. The building was as quiet as death, and I sensed there was no one here. Unless the meeting wrapped up incredibly quickly or they were lying in wait for us, we'd wasted our time.

Marsh ran the flashlight beam over the floor and up a wall and stopped it on the frame of an interior door.

"That's where he was supposed to take the stairs."

He led the way, and I followed him up the dark cement stairs to the second floor. Marsh was careful with the door there, but it didn't make any noise when he carefully opened it and stepped out into a corridor, with more cement floors and a false ceiling above us. The floor hadn't been vacuumed in a long time, and dust motes whirled up under every footstep.

Marsh unclipped his gun holster, and we paused and listened, studying our surroundings closely.

There were more boxes stacked along the hallway, which narrowed the gap so that we had to turn a bit sideways to squeeze through the corridor.

Still absolutely no sign of life.

Our soft-soled shoes barely registered, but we tippy-toed anyway.

At the end of the hallway, the space opened into a coven of spaces, three to be exact, any one of which might be the meeting location.

The open area once again was stacked to the ceiling with more supply boxes.

We stopped and listened for what seemed like an hour, but was probably no more than a minute.

Finally, Marsh pointed his flashlight at the door closest to us. I led the way and pressed my ear against its cold surface.

After another lengthy wait, I shrugged at Marsh, and he nodded.

The door was unlocked, and the room was empty save for more boxes, a small card table, a couple of ripped Naugahyde chairs, a rusty looking refrigerator, and a Coke machine.

The next office was just as empty of life, with its only unique feature being a treadmill.

Behind the door of the third and final office, we again found no life.

But we did find Davis Hunter's dead body alongside that of a young and attractive woman who I recognized, despite the bullet wound that had ripped open the side of her head.

CHAPTER 35

We sat on canvas chairs on the back deck of my boat. The rain had stopped, and the still air was full of a clean ozone smell, tinged with an earthy, oily scent. The half-moon was directly overhead, and there was a smattering of stars, visible through drifting black clouds.

Red was on my lap, purring contentedly as I ran my right hand absently across his back.

My left hand held a small glass of whiskey, a robust old Kentucky bourbon. Marsh was sipping Pierre Ferrand cognac, that he paid for and I kept on hand especially for him. Otherwise, I just flash the fancy bottle to impress my friends.

Something of Lewis Carroll from *Alice* kept flashing across my mind:

If you drink too much from a bottle marked "poison" it is certain to disagree with you sooner or later...

Marsh had used one of his untraceable prepaid cell phones to make the call to the SFPD. His report was curt and to the point. He said there were gunshots, gave the address, and then disconnected the call. He hadn't made the call until after we'd left Treasure Island and were back on Yerba Buena.

As we crossed back over to the 101, we heard, in the distance, police sirens alternating with that weird chirping sound that cop cars make to alert wayward autos.

The dead woman, Katie, the girl I'd seen topless with Hunter in his backyard in Sausalito, had a 9mm Smith & Wesson handgun clutched loosely in her rigid right hand.

The blood from the three visible gun wounds on the bodies was still fresh and oozing. Katie's bullet had torn through the bone and cartilage at the scalp line on the right side of her forehead. There were two visible shots to Davis Hunter's body—one in the middle of his throat that peeled back the flesh like a surgeon's incision, and the other, a small entry hole just above his heart.

We'd probably missed the killers by minutes. They say baseball is a game of luck and timing, but so is life itself. Fate balances on a precarious tightrope.

After fruitlessly searching Hunter's body for his cell phone and wallet, we looked around to make sure we hadn't left a hint of our presence and then hightailed it out of there. The gloves made sure there'd be no fingerprints and rubber slipovers did the same for our shoes.

We had driven back to my boat, fetched our drinks, and settled on the deck without exchanging a word. Finally, after more silent contemplation of the night and the bay, Marsh turned to me and said, "Murder-suicide."

That was obviously the setup, but it was the first time either one of us had mentioned it out loud. It was the only thing that made sense. And yet, at the same time, didn't.

"He probably killed Johnnie, too, didn't he?"

I sipped my whiskey and stared off to the west, over the drifting sailboats, cruisers, and catamarans, and out toward Alcatraz Island. "I can't imagine why, but the evidence certainly points in that direction." I paused and remembered the recording Marsh had played for me earlier in the evening. "What about the tape— Poe talking to Hunter? That alone might be enough to hang him."

"I don't know. Without Hunter's cell phone, which I'm sure has been destroyed by now, I don't know what it's worth."

I wasn't enough of a lawyer to know if a recording disembodied from its source hardware was admissible in a court of law.

"I'll see if there's any precedent. But even if there is, we have to think long and hard before using it," Marsh said, tapping his cognac glass against the arm of his chair. "Maybe we can use it as a bargaining chip to get more information out of Poe, although that, too, might be dangerous to health and well-being."

No doubt.

"But he said it was his building. Why would he kill someone in a property he owned?"

"I have a feeling that it'll turn out that there's no connection between that warehouse and Poe," Marsh said with a tone of resignation.

"But what about all those boxes of supplies?"

"Did you see any labels or indications that they belonged to his casino? I bet it's part of some business that has nothing to do with Poe's various enterprises."

I nodded. "You have to be right." Red sat up, arched his back, and dug his nails into my thighs. I winced and carefully lifted him up and dropped him onto the deck. He gave me a dismissive meow and wandered off toward the back of the boat.

"But I still can't figure out why he'd kill Johnnie and then lead the little girl toward me." I was thinking out loud. "Johnnie was involved with Hunter. Probably a couple years back when the final approvals for the casino were needed. She was either the price for Hunter's cooperation or she was blackmailing him in some way, although I see that as unlikely if Hunter was as besotted with her as he confessed. She may have coaxed him into throwing his vote, or maybe she was just Poe's added insurance." I paused, drank, thought some more.

"I was at the library doing research. and Hunter's vote was the deciding, and—to some reporters—surprising one, as he'd been a vocal casino critic. Poe couldn't bribe him, at least with money, because he was already rich. I'm guessing that Johnnie had pictures or videos of their time together and some of the more kinky activities that floated Hunter's boat but that she never had to use them because Cupid's arrow struck him hard and he'd do anything to please her."

"The course of true love never did run smooth," Marsh said, quoting Shakespeare and taking another sip of overpriced cognac. Then he added, "Everything you say is possible, perhaps probable, of course, but after squeezing everything we could out of Caballo and the Blue Notes and Dr. Wainright and your friends, Maggie and Leonard, there's no way to prove any of it, unless we find Johnnie alive or get Poe to talk. Neither seems remotely likely."

"No matter the legal option of using the recording, we can use it anyway. If he finds out that we have him on tape coaxing Hunter out to his appointment with the grim reaper, it's got to rattle him."

"Didn't your mom ever tell you not to play with fire?"

"Let's find out more about poor Katie. The online paper tomorrow should have information about her, and we should try and find out how she got out to that warehouse because she sure didn't get there with Hunter. Poe probably had her kidnapped and hauled over. Maybe one of her neighbors saw something."

Marsh said, "I'll get somebody out to wherever she lived and see what we can turn up."

"Now we need to plan our approach to Poe and decide what we want from him and what we're willing to do to get it. And, obviously, stage the meeting somewhere that's safe."

"Even if the meeting is secure, afterward there may be no place on Earth that's ever going to be safe again for either of us."

I knew he was right. I didn't know what to do about it, how to avoid Poe's vengeance if we pushed him too far. I thought about Frankie, her grit and determination. She was just a kid who'd already lost too much.

I thought about Dr. Wainright and his poor wife, and the love between them that knew no bounds.

I thought about Hunter and Katie and their awful fate.

I thought about hapless, dead Leonard and poor pitiful Maggie.

We'd come too far. I'd come too far to stop now.

CHAPTER 36

Early the next morning, I was on the back deck of the more stately *Sweet and Sour* having coffee with Alexandra. She had slept overnight on the yacht, babysitting Frankie. Dao and Meiying were in Los Angeles for the weekend at some kind of a conference on opportunities for investment among emerging Asian nations.

Frankie was circling the boat, practicing skateboard tricks.

As Alexandra watched her whirl by, both woman and girl beaming smiles, I finished explaining the situation to her.

"Maybe it's time you got the police involved," she said. "Poe is too dangerous, Max."

"That won't work."

"It might work to save your life," she said.

Frankie skidded to a stop in front of us, kick flipped her board into her hands, and gave a little open-handed flourish. "Ta-da!" she laughed.

We clapped and she bowed.

"Sweetie, you haven't eaten breakfast yet. There are blueberry muffins and bananas on the counter downstairs. Give Red his breakfast and a bowl of milk. Max and I need to talk for a few more minutes, and then I'll come down so we can plan the day."

"Okay," she said, turning away with the skateboard tucked under her arm. She spun back and said, "Can we go to Balls to the Wall this morning? Nick's going to be there."

She was referring to a nearby warehouse converted into a combo laser tag, paintball, and skateboard rink. Nick was her best, and probably only, friend.

"I have lots of errands to run and there might not be—"

"Please. Please. Please!" she cried. "Pretty please. I'll do anything. I haven't seen Nick in years. Please?"

Alexandra laughed, shook her head. "In years? I thought you saw him last Thursday."

"Yeah, but only for a little while. I have so much to tell him. Please?" Her little face wrinkled up into a bursting ball.

"All right. But only for an hour."

"Two hours."

"One hour," Alexandra said firmly.

"And a half," Frankie tried.

"And fifteen minutes," Alexandra conceded, extending her hand.

Frankie smiled, shook it, turned away again. At the cabin door, she stopped, turned around and said, "Mr. Plank...have you...do you...did you find anything out about Johnnie yet?"

I'd been avoiding that topic with her, and now I felt like a heel and a failure. "No. Not yet. But I'm still trying. With a little luck, we'll find out where Johnnie is pretty soon." The words felt weightless, empty.

"Okay. I hope so. Thank you, Mr. Plank." She disappeared down the stairs.

"Goddammit."

"You're doing all you can." Alexandra reached out and touched my knee.

"A fat lot of good that's done her."

"She's something, isn't she?"

I nodded.

"Almost makes you want to..." Alexandra paused, looked out over the line of boats stretching out across Pier 39.

Even though I knew what she was trying to say, I responded, "What?"

"Never mind." She shook it off and said, "So why would getting help from the police not work?"

"What would I tell them? Unless I want to accuse him of being involved in the murders. We have his voice on a third-hand recording. I'm sure his high-priced attorneys will make mincemeat out of that. Plus, he has friends in high places in the city. Friends who owe him favors or allegiance. Or are just plain afraid of him."

"So Superman is going to do this all alone. Confront and threaten the city's most dangerous gangster, to say nothing of his countless minions. I understand you want to help Frankie. So do I. But this is crazy. I don't want to lose you."

"You forget, I'll have Batman with me," I lied.

Alexandra gave me the evil eye. "Marsh is only a man, Max. He'll bleed just like you."

"Don't let him hear you say that."

With a look of pained resignation, she rose to join Frankie downstairs and said, "I am glad Marsh will be with you. And you two better have a good plan, which includes an exit strategy."

I stood up and took her in my arms and whispered, "Don't worry. We do."

What else could I say?

CHAPTER 37

No one knew where Poe really lived.

No one but Marsh.

They were so similar in some ways, particularly their unpredictability and mysterious habits and history.

It turned out that Poe moved among numerous habitats. He had an apartment on the top floor of the casino and a *pied á terre* in Pacific Heights. He owned a Victorian near Golden Gate Park and a loft in Sausalito. He also kept a whole penthouse floor of the Fairmont Hotel on Nob Hill.

And that only counted known residences in the Bay Area.

He also had a fortress-like mansion in Big Sur and a sprawling villa in Beverly Hills.

According to Marsh, he seemed to move among these various residences in no discernible pattern. He might stay at one for a few days, or a week, or even longer sometimes. Or he might move almost every day.

He was either paranoid, or careful, or a little of both.

Or, considering his notoriety and potential list of enemies, just plain damn smart.

Marsh told me he'd employed a small drone with a powerful mini-camera trained on the casino and, whenever possible, Poe himself, for the past few days. Three nights ago, Poe stayed in the casino all night. Two nights ago, he slept on Nob Hill. The same for last night.

Tonight he'd been tracked to the back of the Fairmont Hotel. He'd arrived by helicopter, landing on the roof of the hotel, and then descended a stairwell to the library in the penthouse suite through a secret built-in door that had been designed into the room many years ago. Marsh told me the suite was 6000 square feet and could host up to 130 people for dinner parties. It rented for $15,000 a night. But he probably got a cut rate deal for his long term rental.

Marsh's eye-in-the-sky seemed preposterous, although I knew it was quite possible.

The only thing I really trusted was that if Marsh said Poe was at the Fairmont, then Poe was at the Fairmont.

Marsh asked me if I wanted to make our move tonight.

I told him to check out the place as much as he could and figure out an approach, a plan. If Poe stayed there tomorrow, we'd strike.

If he moved again, we'd reassess.

I didn't like lying to Marsh, any more than I liked telling Alexandra that Batman was going to be my sidekick on this mission.

But neither of them would have let me have my way.

I didn't want to expose Marsh to Poe's forces and revenge. He was a big boy, and he could more than defend himself, but this was different. If Poe wanted someone dead, sooner or later, they stopped breathing.

I'm no hero, but I'd promised the kid, and I was in too deep. I had to know what happened to Johnnie, and my curiosity about the rest of the characters in this tragedy was too intense.

I had a plan, and it even had a slight chance of succeeding.

If it didn't, the fallout would bury me. But, plain and simple, I love Marsh and know he loves me and would lay down his life for me.

I wasn't going to give him the chance.

CHAPTER 38

The Fairmont, sitting atop Nob Hill, is one of San Francisco's oldest establishments for the powerful and wealthy. And those yearning to join them.

I'd been there a few times, most memorably for my high school junior prom, where Jeanette Peterson and I had Shirley Temples in the chez cheesy Tonga Room and oohed and ahhed about the indoor rain showers and the band floating on a barge in a swimming pool near the Tiki bar.

I'd impressed her so much by taking her there that she graced me with my first kiss that night. More than one, to be precise.

The outside of the massive edifice looked much like city hall, and its Beaux-Arts interior style is nothing if not eye-catching.

Alas, I wasn't going to get the chance to admire the lobby and public rooms, as I'd decided the only feasible way past Poe's defenses was the one he'd least expect: mimicking his own entry.

Marsh rented a helicopter every now and then and had a pilot on retainer. I knew the guy, Daryl, pretty well. He was a sixty-year-old Vietnam vet. I'd contacted him right after Marsh told me where Poe was sleeping tonight, and promised to double his rate if he'd take me to the Fairmont. I got him to promise not to tell my friend in advance. There'd be plenty of time for Marsh to be pissed at me afterward. If I survived.

So, at just after 10 p.m., the helicopter burst through a flock of low lying clouds and veered up out of the Bay and past the Trans-America pyramid. In less than a minute, we were circling the Fairmont, and I was out the cockpit door, balancing on the landing skids. The engine's roar and the thumping of the rotors exploded in my ears, deafening me.

Daryl dropped down close to the helicopter pad, but didn't land, hovering fifteen feet from touchdown.

I didn't pause a moment, waved a quick goodbye to Daryl, and fell onto the balcony, hitting hard, tumbling end over end before jumping back up to a crouch. My feet hurt, my shins and hands were bruised, but all in all, in better shape than I'd feared.

The helicopter banked sharply and streaked back out across the Bay.

I was on my own now, the only escape route down through the penthouse and the hotel.

As the thumping drone of the 'copter disappeared, I stood motionless, listening for any hint of alarm or human approach.

I took in the beautiful stone mosaic flooring, several potted plants, a small fountain, the black metal table, and four cushioned chairs overlooking the stunning view of the financial district and the Bay.

Money did have its privileges.

I listened intently. Other than street sounds from far below and the strong wind whistling in my ears, the gentle tinkling of the fountain, and the cooing sounds of some nearby pigeons, I couldn't sense any danger.

I knew it was questionable but hoped that our quick arrival and departure might go unnoticed by the occupants of the penthouse suite on the eighth floor below me.

I moved toward an alcove and a door that Marsh had told me led down to the penthouse.

I was relying on a lot of suppositions and hoping for blind luck.

I tried the doorknob.

It gave under my hand.

Bingo.

When I swung it open, I found a long winding red carpeted staircase.

I also found Angelique with a pistol in her hand pointed directly at my chest.

CHAPTER 39

S he seemed no happier to see me than she had when she'd
served me espresso back at the casino.
She hadn't spoken a single word to me the last time we
met, but she remedied that immediately.

"We've been expecting you."

The accent had a Caribbean vibe to it, perhaps Haitian. She
exuded a musky, cinnamon scent. She still looked formidable and
gorgeous. She had sultry, silvery, near almond-shaped eyes that
packed a wallop.

I smiled at her, trying to keep my composure.

She backed me up with a wave of the gun and carefully
stepped behind me and onto the balcony.

Then she shoved the barrel of the gun against my back and
escorted me over to the comfy chairs surrounding the steel table.
She bid me sit down, and I did, picking the chair with the
best view.

A cell appeared in her hand, and a moment later, she spoke
into it.

"Li fè."

The word sounded like French with a twist. Perhaps Haitian Creole?

It also sounded close to "Life," which, ridiculously, gave me a little feeling of hope.

Five minutes later, Poe joined me at the table, sitting with his back to the view. She handed him the gun and then searched me thoroughly from head to toe, looking, I assumed, for any hint of a weapon or a wire. Her lovely hands, with their long elegant fingers, lingered in places both innocuous and intimate.

When she finished, I shimmied my shoulders and said, "Thank you so much."

She ignored me and took the gun back from Poe, holstering it on her back. She circled the table and positioned herself somewhere behind my chair.

I guess they weren't too worried about what I'd do.

Maybe the half-dozen armed men lurking near the stairwell had something to do with it.

Before he spoke, Poe let out a long exasperated sigh to let me know he'd reached the limits of his patience.

"I don't understand you."

"That's not the first time I've heard that complaint."

He gave me a look that told me humor wasn't going to serve me well here.

"Sorry to drop in on you like this." I couldn't help myself. Really, I never can.

Poe nodded at Angelique. Faster than I could blink, she was behind me. I quickly realized she was familiar with some of the same pressure points as Marsh.

I winced, then growled, then whimpered. It was embarrassing.

Poe nodded again, and she stepped back.

"Before I leave you to Angelique, you have one chance to explain yourself. I wouldn't waste it, were I you. You've interrupted my evening. I've warned you repeatedly. It won't take her long to make you wish you'd never been born."

With those inspirational words, I decided to get right to the point.

"I was at the warehouse the other night when Hunter and his lover were murdered."

Now I had his full attention.

"Careful, Plank," he said, and the tone of his voice, along with Angelique lurking close behind me, sent a jolt of electricity from my toes to the hairs on top of my head.

"I asked this before, and I'm asking again right now. Did you kill Johnnie?"

I flinched as Angelique's fingers touched my shoulder.

"Is there anything else?" Poe said, feigning boredom.

It was now or never, and never certainly was an attractive option with Angelique threatening havoc. "We have a recording, taken from Hunter's cell phone, of you talking with him. We have him threatening you. And, in turn, the tape exposes you setting up the meeting at the warehouse."

Poe was on his feet, in my face, roaring, "You fucking shit stain. Are you out of your mind?"

He slapped me hard across my cheek with the back of his hand.

My head rocked to the side, but I managed to stay in the chair. The whole right side of my face tingled and flushed with blood. My teeth ached. Maybe that's because I was clenching them in humiliation and anger.

His outburst shocked me. Over the years, I'd had a fair number of encounters with him and never seen him lose his serene composure. I wasn't the only one taken aback. Angelique had removed her hand from me and stepped away. I sensed indecision in her movement.

Poe was standing above me with his fists clenched. I looked up into his eyes and, for a brief moment, saw clearly the cold-blooded killer that he was.

He took a step back, sat back down, shook his head, smirked. "I have to hand it to you. You're like a tick that keeps burrowing and burrowing. Damn annoying but impossible to ignore."

I took a deep breath before speaking. "I'm not trying to annoy you or get you, Poe. Even if you had Hunter and Kate killed. Even if you were somehow responsible for Johnnie's disappearance, I know that I can't bring you down." I paused, straightened myself up in my seat, massaged my bruised cheek. "But I'm trying to help that little girl. That's what I don't get. You told her to come see me. In a way, you could say I'm working for you, or at least doing what you expected me to do. Just trying to follow all of the leads I can to find the girl's sister. It's not my fault that a lot of the leads seem to somehow circle back to you. Maybe it's just coincidence..." I let my voice trail off. I didn't believe that for a second but knew I was on a tightrope without a net.

The pigeons still cooed from a dark corner of the building. The muffled sounds of street life—humming cars, ethereal voices, the ratcheting bump and whir of street cars—echoed from far beneath us.

I was just about to speak again when Poe broke his silence. When I looked into his face, something had changed, and so had his voice. It was soft now, a little uncertain. "I didn't have anything to do with Johnnie's disappearance. I don't know what happened to her. You'd never understand our relationship. Despite her problems, she was something. Unique, charismatic, strong. Impossibly attractive. But flawed in so many ways. And unlucky. Goddamn unlucky."

If there was one thing sure that I'd gotten out of this investigation, it was the wish that I'd had the chance to meet Johnnie, an enigma that would probably never be solved by any mere man.

Poe continued. "I sent the little girl to you because I care about her and Johnnie. You can believe that or not. I don't care. But I know what you're like, for good or bad. Thought you were the man for the job. I knew the risk with you. I made a mistake. I won't make it again."

"Then why are you upset with me doing my job?" I was profoundly disappointed that I'd be getting no more referrals from him.

Poe drummed his fingers on the table top. "There are lines. You keep on stepping over them. Keep me out of this. I run a big business that's very important to the city and the state and the people. My name has to stay out of the papers."

"Okay. I believe that you had nothing to do with Johnnie's disappearance. But you are involved with the Blue Notes. You had Caballo's men come after me looking for her computer. Why?"

"I didn't..." He stopped, looked down, leaned over the glass table, flattening his hands along its surface. "That was to protect Hunter. I didn't even know she was still involved with him. If I had..." He hesitated, looked off to the side, considering how much to say.

"But you used her against him. To make sure he voted for the casino." I knew I was treading in dangerous waters again.

He gave me a sharp look but didn't strike out. "I introduced them at a party a few years back. Hunter was always looking for something on the side. His wife is a bitch. A rich one, but still a bitch."

"So you thought she might...persuade him to—"

"I introduced them. Period. End of sentence and story."

"I assume what happened to Hunter and Katie are not up for discussion either?"

"You assume correctly."

I almost asked how he snatched Katie and got her to the warehouse, but really, for a man like Poe, it was undoubtedly as easy as a finger snap. It didn't really matter how it happened. Hunter had become a little unhinged and represented a threat that had to be eliminated. The tidy murder-suicide setup made it easy for the police and powers that be to wrap it up quickly. No muss and fuss. Another tragic tale of lust and betrayal and loveless marriage among the rich and powerful.

The newspapers and online media were full of screaming headlines, but the emphasis was on the tryst between the lovers and the sad plight of the poor, prominent widow. The police were said to be working diligently to uncover any possible clues or alternate explanations, but it was really an open and shut case. The only dissenting voice was the one that Marsh had recorded of Poe, himself, coaxing the victims to their date with death. Unless we used it against him, there was no chance he would ever be linked to the murders.

"I have only one more question. You said you had a couple of guys pay a visit to Leonard to dissuade him from dealing in...delicate areas that might get him into trouble. I assume that somehow he might have found out about Johnnie's involvement with Wainright, and, more importantly, Hunter, and was about to apply pressure to them to extort money."

Poe gave me a long, noncommittal look. I thought he wasn't going to answer at all, but eventually he responded. "That's about right. Leonard was trying to involve himself in matters well above his capacities. He was a third-rate hustler. A loser with an anchor around his neck. I don't know how he found out about Hunter's involvement with Johnnie, but fortunately, he opened his mouth to some of his buddies and it got back to us. I never had a chance to talk to Johnnie about it, but I was doing it for her as much as Hunter."

And yourself, I thought. Then something he said hit me like a badly plucked guitar string. "You mentioned an anchor around Leonard's neck. What does that mean?"

"What else? That woman of his. She'd gotten pregnant. She

was a dope head, a heavy pot user from what I've been told. Spacey, but crazy about Leonard, I guess. Hard to imagine what she saw in him. She was so much younger and not half bad looking, from the picture I saw."

I sat there mulling his words over in my mind for a few moments, trying to make sense of it.

When it hit me, it struck with the force of a hammer blow.

With a sickening feeling in the pit of my stomach, I suddenly knew what had happened to Johnnie.

I didn't want to be there anymore. I felt dirty and complicit. I needed a long, hot shower and a stiff drink before I faced what I needed to confront.

"Can I go now?" I said, leveling my gaze at Poe.

"Don't you want to have it out with Angelique first?" Poe said with a straight face.

"I'd like nothing more, but I have a feeling that our conception of ways and means might be totally contradictory."

Poe laughed for a little too long.

"The only way you'll avoid unpleasantness is by promising to give me the source recordings from Hunter's cell phone. All of them, including any copies. I believe this is an unnecessary step as they pose no real threat. Nevertheless, I'd feel better were they not in your possession."

I agreed, and Angelique escorted me down the stairs, through the unbelievably opulent penthouse, and down a private elevator to the lobby of the Fairmont. Neither of us spoke a word. I had a feeling that we'd only postponed the inevitable and that a confrontation between us would happen sooner or later.

Outside, I stood on the curb for a long time, ignoring the people and cars, the shouts and laughs, the whole damn noisy world swirling around me.

Finally, knowing there was no way I could sleep or do anything else, I hailed a cab and gave him the address.

CHAPTER 40

I was back on that front porch jungle, one last time.

I was sure I wouldn't ever step foot here again after tonight.

The smell was still pungent, weedy, the vanilla still noticeable. But I sensed putrefaction, all the wildflowers going to seed.

Maybe it was just me.

I'd knocked twice then rang the bell.

I waited. I could hear rustling at the back of the house.

Maggie finally answered, wearing a long t-shirt, one of Leonard's, the Grateful Dead huddled around a campfire. Jerry Garcia's grizzled features smiled out at the world in bemusement. He always seemed a little baffled to me, a byproduct of all the drugs he'd ingested.

She didn't look surprised to see me. She didn't say a word but stepped back inside and disappeared into the front room. I entered the house and gently closed the door behind me.

It smelled worse inside. The air was stale. I'd guess a window hadn't been opened in days. It felt like everything in that house was rotting.

I joined Maggie in the front room, sitting on an uncomfortable chair, made out of cheap wood, in front of a bean bag across from where she sat on a decrepit love seat. She sat with her hands resting on her knees and her eyes cast to the floor.

My mind had been a blank on the ride over, and now I took my time composing my thoughts, my questions. My investigation was ending right about where it had started.

It seemed surprising, but thinking about it right then and there, it all made a horrific kind of sense. So much had happened. Johnnie's life had been so involved with so many weak and/or troubled and dangerous men. There were so many motives and cross purposes that it shouldn't have been so surprising that the truth—so evident now—had been so hard to cull out from the entanglements. As difficult as finding a single snapdragon in that tropical jungle that Maggie cultivated and let run wild on her front porch.

"Maggie, tell me what happened when you told Leonard you were pregnant."

She hardly reacted. There was no alarm or protest in her voice, just a depressing resignation. "He got mad at me. For allowing it to happen. I claimed it was an accident." Suddenly, a pathetic sob escaped her throat, but she strangled it, gasped, gathered herself. "He didn't know I'd stopped taking the pill."

"Why?" I said.

She looked up at me for the first time, a look of stunned puzzlement on her face. "To make him see."

She searched my face for understanding.

"Make him see what, Maggie?"

"See how much I loved him. How much I cared. See how she would never love him in the same way." She looked away awkwardly, having exposed herself completely.

"Did he ever express a desire for a child?"

"No," she answered quickly. "No, but I could tell. I knew it would bind us like nothing else. He was obsessed with her. Men can't help themselves with a woman like her. She used him. I tried to tell her...I..." She sobbed again, covering her eyes with trembling hands.

"Maggie..."

"She could have just about any man she wanted. I told her Leonard was all I had. I told her I'd do anything, give her money, if she'd just leave him be."

The house was deathly quiet, just rotting away moment after moment.

I didn't want to hear the answer to my next question, but I had to ask it.

"How did she respond?"

"She said she'd only..." she stopped, winced, her face scrunched in anguish, "...been with him once. She said she had no interest in him, other than the business. She said I could have him." She paused, wiped the tears from her face. "That made me mad. She wouldn't leave. She said as soon as she made enough money, she'd find a better place for her and Frankie, but she had nowhere to go. In the meantime, he was crazy about her. I couldn't take it. I didn't know what to do. I stopped taking the pill. We hadn't made love for months. I got him to drinking, and then I seduced him." She paused again, then said, "I got pregnant."

"When did you tell him?"

"I didn't, not at first. I told Johnnie first. I told her the night when Leonard was away, visiting his parents in Bakersfield. He did that once a year. Frankie was out, too. With a friend, I think."

"What did Johnnie say?"

"She told me how stupid I was. How Leonard was a weak man and would never be a good father or husband. I told her she had to leave right then and there. I told her to get out..."

She stopped and I waited.

After a while, Maggie continued. "She refused. She laughed. I don't why. I think I took it the wrong way, maybe she wasn't ridiculing me. But it made me feel pathetic. I slapped her, and she hit me back. We fought. I picked up a rock. It was just sitting on the table. A piece of the stupid art she collected. I don't even know what it was supposed to be. It looked like a shiny rock to me...."

She paused again. And again, I remained silent.

"...I didn't mean to. She was so angry. Something about the money she was owed. I was out of my mind with fear of losing Leonard. I hit her once, on the side of her head, and she fell. Her face hit the table, and she groaned and made a strange gurgling sound in her throat. Then she stopped making any noise. I dropped beside her and told her I was sorry, so sorry...but her eyes didn't see me. They didn't see anything. She didn't have a pulse. I didn't know what to do."

She stopped and stared at her trembling hands.

"What happened next?" I said gently.

"I was out of my mind. I thought about calling the police, but I couldn't let my baby grow up with me in jail. So I dragged her body down into the garage and managed to get it into the trunk of my car. It seemed impossible. I didn't think I could do it. But you know what they say about the power and strength of a mother protecting her child..." She closed her eyes and in a whisper said, "Maybe that was it.

"I put a shovel in the trunk with her, and then I drove out of the city. I didn't know where I was going. I was only thinking about my baby and Leonard. I ended up heading north, into the redwoods, Muir Woods. Finally, I found a spot. It was late and very dark, and there was no one else there. I drove the car off the road into the woods. I found some muddy soil beneath a tree and thick bushes. I dug a hole as deep as I could. It took me a long time. Hours, I think. I buried her. I thought it was a good place because it wasn't anywhere that hikers or campers were likely to be. I guess I was right because she hasn't been found yet."

I detected a hint of satisfaction in her voice, and it disturbed me even more than her words.

I waited for her to finish and then asked, "You said Leonard was angry with you about the baby when you told him. What happened?"

"He saw how upset I was. But he told me he couldn't be a father. Not then. Not ever. He told me I had to get an abortion." She paused, gathering herself. "Do you know what that did to me? What I had done for him and for the baby?" She looked at me as if she expected an answer.

I stared into her eyes and lowered my chin slightly, acknowledging her.

"But he insisted. Told me he'd leave me and the baby if I kept it. When he said that, something broke inside me. He found me a clinic online and told me to get over there the next day. He said it wasn't a big deal. In a few days, I'd forget all about it."

"What did you do?"

"I went to the clinic the next day. I had the abortion."

"Maggie, I don't know what—"

"But when I killed my baby, our baby, I killed us. The idea of us. The hope of me and Leonard."

And with that, another light bulb popped on in my mind. I waited for it to settle and then said, "How did you manage to give him an overdose?"

It took her a long time to answer. "He didn't do drugs, other than some pot. But he did drink. I put some Benadryl in his wine, and he passed out. Then I injected him with some of the stuff he sells on the street."

And that was it. If there was one victim, other than Frankie, in this whole sordid affair, I'd thought it was Maggie.

But it turned out that she was the murderer.

So why was it that I still thought of her as a victim?

WE SAT IN SILENCE FOR A LONG WHILE AFTER SHE FINISHED speaking. I expected her to ask me to keep her secrets to myself, but she didn't. I think she was beyond caring about her own life.

I left her there and didn't call the police until I got back to my boat.

I called a detective I knew by the name of Spence and told him what I knew, leaving out much of the related trouble. I didn't mention Poe or the Blue Notes or Caballo or Wainright or Davis Hunter.

None of that mattered now.

The killer was found and the simple, clean story would be told on the front page of the *San Francisco Examiner.*

Another tale of lust, betrayal, and murder.

I sat on my back deck, staring out into the dark night, with a drink in my hand until I couldn't keep my eyes open.

Then I went to bed.

CHAPTER 41

"Uncle Max," Jen shouted from the dance floor. "Come dance with the bride."

I looked up from my plate of crab legs and roasted potatoes and found her waving at me. I watched her bounce and gyrate with her dad in a crowd of people in the cleared out family room. The band was playing a pretty fair rendition of Prince's, "When Doves Cry."

Bo waved at me, too, and I waved back.

Jen was as beautiful and young as her white dress.

Eighteen, married, and radiant in her happiness.

A magnificent and foolish young woman, but what the hell? Her new hubby was a lucky bastard, and I hoped he realized it and treated her right. He'd better, or he'd have Bo—and me—to deal with.

The kid, the groom, looked overmatched and clueless, but maybe there was more there than met the eye. The wedding at a nearby Catholic Church had been lovely, and Alexandra's hand clutched mine with emotion a couple of times during the ceremony.

"C'mon, Uncle Max!" She smiled and urged me over with a shimmy of her shoulders.

I held up a hand and shouted back. "I will. Next dance." I was sure that Bo was the one coaxing her to get me on the dance floor.

Jen wagged her finger at me, pursed her lips in disapproval, and went back to her wild bouncing.

Marsh and Tom, reunited for the moment, were sitting at my table. They looked resplendent in white tuxedos.

Marsh had gotten over his anger with me, but he told me if I ever tried a stunt like confronting Poe without telling him again, he'd kill me himself.

It was a little over a month since I'd left Maggie's house, and a lot had happened.

She'd been charged with two murders and was being held under a suicide watch in the county jail. California had no death penalty, but I thought that sooner or later she'd take her own life. What she'd done, what had been done to her, was soul destroying, and I doubted she had the resources to recover.

Dr. Wainright had called me a week ago to tell me that his wife had passed away, and to thank me for not turning him in.

I expressed my condolences while feeling ashamed of his thanks.

The local media buzz about the murders of Hunter Davis and Katie had quieted some. Hunter's wife was rumored to be at her villa in France, and no one seemed to know when or whether she'd ever return. The police investigation was ongoing, but no one expected anything to come of it.

Poe's casino had reported record profits, which meant record revenue for the city and county of San Francisco and the state of California.

I'd visited Poe three weeks ago, making sure to set up a formal appointment with his people in advance. At that meeting, I gave him the audio recording from Hunter's cell phone. He seemed as shocked as anyone to find out that Maggie had killed both Johnnie and Leonard.

Poe offered me money for Frankie. I turned him down.

Angelique was at the meeting, too, but she didn't say a word to me.

A couple of weeks back, there'd been a story in the paper about a gang shooting in the Mission. Two gang members had been caught in the crossfire during some kind of a dustup. A drug deal gone wrong.

The two men, Vince and Scooter, had been killed.

The police were trying to get to the bottom of it and had arrested a couple of suspects, but the whole affair was murky. There was some mention of the Blue Notes and their activities, but I'd seen no follow up to the story.

I'd thought about Frankie a lot over the past few weeks. One of the hardest things I'd ever had to do was tell her that her sister was dead. It was a good thing I had Alexandra to help. She'd been a champ with the grieving girl since then.

Alexandra returned to our table and sat beside me. She'd been down to visit Frankie in the basement, where Bo had set up a special area for the kids, including a large inflatable bouncer and a magician—a friend of ours, another ex-rock and roll musician trying to go semi-legit.

She leaned over and gave me a big kiss on the lips. When she pulled away, her eyes were dancing and intense. "I love her, Max."

"Yes, I know."

"If they can't find any other relatives, I want to adopt her."

I nodded.

"Will you help me?" she asked, and put her hand on my knee.

Before I could answer, Jen grabbed my hands and pulled me to my feet. "It's your turn, Uncle Max," she cried and dragged me onto the dance floor.

AUTHOR NOTE

Hello Dear Reader,

You made it to the end of the book and I sure hope you enjoyed the journey.

Thanks for giving me your valuable time. I surely appreciate it.

What I would also greatly appreciate is if you could give other readers the benefit of your experience. Could you take a few moments to go to Amazon and leave an honest review?

Reviews are essential for others to discover my work and for me to keep telling stories.

Thank you!!!

ABOUT THE AUTHOR

Robert Bucchianeri is the author of the Max Plank Mystery Series along with the suspense thriller, Between a Smile and a Tear, the psychological thriller, Ransom Dreams, the rock n'roll mystery, Acapella Blues, as well as the sunlit noir, Love Stings. He is also the author of the novella, Jet: The Fortress, an espionage thriller. Along with his wife, son and wonder dog, Buddy, he resides, mostly, on Cape Cod.

For More Information
https://rjbucchianeri.com

MORE MAX PLANK COMING SOON

Book 1 Stray Cat Blues
Book 2 The Ties That Bind
Book 3 Devil's Arcade

On Pre-Order Soon

ALSO BY ROBERT BUCCHIANERI

Click on Title for more information:

Mystery Thriller Triple Pack

Between a Smile and a Tear

Ransom Dreams

Acapella Blues

The Fortress

Love Stings

Young Adult Action/Adventure:

Django Jagger & The Mirror of the Moon

Django Jagger & The People of Darkness